James Johnston

Missionary Landscapes in the Dark Continent

Vol. 1

James Johnston

Missionary Landscapes in the Dark Continent
Vol. 1

ISBN/EAN: 9783337404062

Printed in Europe, USA, Canada, Australia, Japan

Cover: Foto ©Andreas Hilbeck / pixelio.de

More available books at **www.hansebooks.com**

MISSIONARY LANDSCAPES

IN THE

DARK CONTINENT

BY

REV. JAMES JOHNSTON, A.T.S.

AUTHOR OF "MISSIONARY POINTS AND PICTURES," ETC.

PREFACE.

In the present volume the author has sketch-
ed in outline a few of the notably fascinating
African spheres where the missionary vanguards
have established their outposts. The triumphs
achieved by these spiritual pioneers merit wide
and generous appreciation in all lands. Against
the two oppressive shadows of native life in
Africa : heathenism and slavery, they have un-
swervingly measured their strength, prowess,
and Christian chivalry. Plunging into pathless
wilds, grappling with the densest ignorance,
combating the most degrading forms of idol-
atry, and steadfastly resisting the horrors of
tribal savagery, these knight-errants of heaven
have placed the feet of Africa's dusky children
upon

     . . . . " The great world's altar-stairs,
That slope through darkness up to God."

To the missionary's self-abnegating and prolonged toils living monuments bear eloquent testimony.

His vocation no longer calls for an apology to the world. The missionary has translated the claims of foreign missions from the realm of speculation and opinion into the region of fact and history, by demonstrating that the negro of the lowest aboriginal type is capable of being raised to "heights of mental and moral glory." As eminently, the missionary is an international ally of science, commerce, statesmanship, and civilisation. When Dr. Moffat spoke on African Missions in the Nave of Westminster Abbey, November 30, 1875, he made the remark that, " Missionaries to a barbarian people deserve a vote of thanks from the commercial world." Without war-axe, spear, or sword, they have been the trader's patron and chief friend.

These ensigns of the Gospel have displayed sanctified courage, and something of the high and noble life of such crusaders as Mackay, Coillard, Laws, Steere, Hore, Arnot, the Comb-

ers, Grenfell, Crowther, Wilmot-Brooke, and
others, is narrated in the following pages.
Their Spartan deeds, stamped on the plains of
the Dark Continent, have stirred the admiration of the Christian nations. For the sake of
neglected and down-trodden Africa, missionary
martyrdoms present an unparalleled record;
heroic spirits having served and fallen in legion,
whose dust lies in the lonely, scattered "God's
Acres" on Africa's shores.

Glowingly said Henry Ward Beecher of the
missionary character: "The man who under-
takes to lift the globe in the sympathy of
Christ who said, ' The field is the world '; the
man who goes out of his parish, and out of his
town, and out of his nation, and goes into the
great stream of universal humanity—that is
the man who follows Christ." In a similar,
impassioned vein Canon Liddon at St. Paul's
Cathedral, alluding to the endeavour of missionaries to plant the standard of the Cross among
African races observed that, by supporting so
grand an object: " Nothing was more truly
Christian and philanthropic, or more worthy

of men who hope to have a part in the resurrection to Eternal Life." By the imperishable victories of missions concerning which fresh and reliable information will be supplied in this work, a loftier enthusiasm is being enkindled for the sacred cause.

The customs, languages, characteristics, and pursuits of the native tribes, and of several portions of the African Continent occupied by the missionaries, have been carefully pourtrayed. A hearty recognition has been accorded to Africa's explorers and discoverers ; a class of heroes, second only to the missionary, on the roll of honour. From the days of Bruce, Mungo Park, and Clapperton, to the time of Burton, Livingstone, "the king of African pioneers," Speke, Grant, Stanley, and Cameron, celebrated travellers have towered in the van, in drawing aside the veil which has shrouded the interior of that immense country. "Daring, always daring," the soldier of exploration penetrating its mystery and vastness has incited the missionary to pitch his tent amid the myriads of poor savages in the heart of Darkest Africa. In breaking through the confines of a land of impenetrable silence the missionary and the explorer have been comrades, august rivals.

Of the broad features of African geography an exact knowledge is of recent date. Only thirty-five years have elapsed since the mighty prize of the source of the Nile was wrested, and, within the last thirty years,—a golden age of discovery,—more has been done for the reclamation of the "Lost Continent" than in the previous 3,300 years. To remove the pall of ignorance which hung over the depths of Central Africa illustrious bodies of exploring parties have exhibited dauntless resolution, intrepid spirit, boundless resource, and vast enterprise ; nor has any other continent claimed so many gallant victims ere its secrets were disclosed. Through the services of these pacific invaders civilisation is beginning to shed its illuminating rays over the dark places of Africa, and Christianity to write its name upon the forehead of African humanity.

In prophetic tones a great missionary has

declared, "Africa will be saved"; and, with her emancipation, the demon of slavery, that remnant of centuries of tyranny and barbarism, will finally be driven from her coasts.

ENGLAND, 1892.

CONTENTS.

NYASA, "THE LAKE OF THE STARS."

NYASA, "THE LAKE OF THE STARS."

A DEEPENING interest gathers around Lake
Nyasa the shores of which were surveyed, less
than thirty years ago, for missionary aggression,
by the Rev. James Stewart, at the request of the
Free Church of Scotland. In face of the recurring
slave wars he intimated that any immediate mission inauguration would be futile. Following
Livingstone's death, occurring on the 4th of
May, 1873, Mr. Stewart, who had in the meantime been appointed head of Lovedale College,
South Africa, propounded in 1874 a fresh
scheme. These views were shared by Mr.
Young, R.N., author of " Nyasa," also a notable
explorer, and, in 1875, this pioneer made the
first circumnavigation of Lake Nyasa which
was discovered to have a length of 350 miles, a
breadth averaging from 16 to 60 miles, and lying in a remarkable hollow of the surrounding

tableland, 1,520 feet above the sea-level. The Free Church then arose with courageous aim to publish light and liberty throughout Nyasaland in obedience to the Master's commission, in response to Livingstone's last prayer, and in compassion for Africa's benighted humanity.

The resolve of the Free Church was countenanced and supported unitedly by the Reformed Presbyterian, the Established, and United Presbyterian churches of Scotland. A year later the Church of Scotland founded its prosperous mission in the Shiré Highlands, above the Murchison Cataracts, at Blantyre,—named after the Lanarkshire village where David Livingstone was born. Two adjacent stations were subsequently erected at Domasi and Chirazulo. Supplied with a score of European and five native missionaries the Blantyre Mission has done effective industrial, evangelistic, and medical service, and likewise conducted school-training in excellent style. Its current yearly outlay amounts to £4,000, and upon the entire working of the mission £40,000 has been spent. Among the honoured names on the Mission staff, Dr. C. Scott, the eminent principal, and Mr. Hetherington, are well-known representatives. At Blantyre to-day stands the finest ecclesiastical edifice between the two extremes of Egypt and Cape Colony, recently built by native labour under European direction.

Planted in the healthiest of situations the Blantyre Mission has been less exposed to climatic perils than the Livingstonia Mission which has suffered the heaviest losses at its advanced outposts. Lately this immunity enjoyed at Blantyre through 15 years of arduous and occasionally perilous labours, ended. Within a brief period of three months in 1891 three of the missionaries were fatally stricken. If not martyrs in the ordinary sense of the name, the story of their lives and deaths nevertheless places them in the rank of the noblest heroes. The trio of Scotsmen, Henry Henderson, Dr. John Bowie, and Robert Cleland, were all students of the University of Edinburgh. To Mr. Henderson belongs the honour of having chosen the site of the Blantyre Mission. A man of delicate tact in winning native confidence, en-

dued with a genuine missionary instinct and
ideal and, of an energy so untiring, that the
natives described him, "the man that never
sleeps." At Quillimane, on the 12th of February, 1891, Mr. Henderson died of fever, his
health shattered by hardships and his spirit
crushed by the death of his wife and child from
diphtheria, a few days previously. The memory
of this pioneer missionary has been preserved
by his old college friends, Lord President Rob-
ertson and Lord Stormonth-Darling, who have
erected a chaste tablet at Kinclaven, "to commemorate in the church of his native parish
a life of enterprise, gentleness, courage, self-
denial, and absolute devotion to the service of
Almighty God." Dr. Bowie, the medical missionary, after achieving a brilliant university
career and obtaining a lucrative practice in
London, offered himself in 1887 for the Blantyre Mission. To receive the medical skill of
the good surgeon during his brief ministry of
healing in the Shiré Highlands the afflicted
natives came in crowds. Of the doctor's kindly
attention to the lowliest African touching in-

cidents are related, and, very pitiful are the circumstances which terminated his devoted life. Ere quite recovering from influenza he performed the operation of tracheotomy on his sister's child attacked by diphtheria. Bravely running all risks he repeatedly sucked the dangerous tube which only gave temporary relief to the child. Within twelve hours the little sufferer died. Immediately following the child's funeral, its bereaved mother, Mrs. Henderson, was seized by the disease, and Dr. Bowie rising from a sick-bed attempted to save her life by means of tracheotomy. The dreaded foe had made too rapid progress on his sister's constitution, and in a short time Mrs. Henderson passed away, her remains being laid to rest beside those of her dear child. And then the same virulent assailant attacked the self-abnegated brother, and for him—" The long self-sacrifice of life is o'er."

The third of this group, Robert Cleland, a Coatbridge engineer in his youthful days, became the first missionary on Mount Milanje, about four days' journey from the Blantyre headquarters. To have the joy of being classed a missionary to the heathen, was an " objective " for which he had laboriously toiled, and had his life, brief, yet fruitful, been prolonged, there was promise of high achievements. An eloquent portraiture sets Cleland and his brother-missionaries before the world as "unwavering in determination, unfailing in their faith in God, and unwearying in their devotion to Africa, and their love for the African," the study of whose careers must incite like-minded servants of Christ to take up the standards which have fallen from their consecrated hands.

By the Free Church of Scotland the Livingstonia Mission was originally established at Cape Maclear, at the south end of Lake Nyasa, a settlement by and by practically abandoned on account of the deadly malaria rising from the imprisoned poisonous agents in the dense soil and undrained marshy plains. In its place, Bandawè, lat. 12°, half-way up the west coast of the lake was chosen, and, from *five* centres the Livingstonia Mission has scattered heavenly rays. Over the growing organizations presides the Rev. Dr. Laws, whom Consul Johnston characterizes the greatest man hitherto known in Nyasa-land. On the eve of his furlough in 1892 he had been toiling, with slight intermission, for sixteen years in Central Africa, directing the policy and expansion of the Mission. With Livingstone and Steere he may be bracketed, and, as signally, merits the praise of Christendom. It was in 1877 that he explored a part of the western shore in company with Dr. Stewart of Scottish renown. A year afterwards Dr. Laws, joined by the late Mr. James Stewart, C.E., made a journey of 700 miles along the southern and westerly skirts of the lake and the hill country beyond. The doctor's inexhaustible activity has been marked by medical services, the direction of schools, building of stations, negotiations with fierce tribes, pastoral engagements and invaluable literary undertakings. At Bandawè alone, 7,000 medical cases were treated in 1887, and in the respective schools nearly two thousand children are getting instruction. Advance is everywhere visible in spite of obstacles which arise from fifteen different tribes speaking as many languages, with minor varying dialects. The Chirenji, Chitonga, Chigunda, and Angoni tongues have been reduced to writing, and of the sixteen publications in the speech of the natives, gospels, hymns, dictionaries, and primers have chief attention. It is some years since the entire New Testament was translated into Chinyanja, and one of the latest linguistical triumphs is the completion of the Chinyanja Dictionary, a scholarly volume of 231 pages, executed by Dr. Laws, amid the raids of slave marauders, tribal warfare, Arab insurrections, and the vicissitudes attending the founding and supervision of new stations. Conquests of this order make the doctor a leader by whose missionary apostleship the Gospel has been marvellously glorified.

On the Nyasa field the stations comprise Bandawè, Mombera's, Chineyera, Chirenji, Chinga, Cape Maclear, Chikusi's, Malindu, and Chewere's—fifty miles west of Lake Nyasa. Prospective stations are afoot at Karonga's, at the north end of Nyasa, renowned as a trading depôt of the African Lakes Company, which the Arabs failed to capture at the time of Captain Lugard's defence; and at Ukukwi or Kararamuka, in a fascinatingly situated forest-clad country to the northeast of the lake, where the Moravians are opening a mission. Thirty-one workers are enrolled on the Free Church staff, including seven ordained medical missionaries, nine artisans and teachers, and a dozen native evangelists. The Dutch Reformed Church at Stellenbosch, South Africa, is now warmly co-operating in the extensions of the Livingstonia Mission, upon which a sum of £60,000 in all, has been expended, and about £5,000 per annum devoted to this spiritually crowned enterprise.

From a holiday ramble which the Rev. Lawrence Scott a North of England clergyman made in Central Africa, in 1888, with some contempt for perils and fatigues, in order to visit a brother-in-law, to carry out a botanical expedition, and, to benefit his fellow-creatures in those far-off regions, realistic glimpses at first hand were obtained of the native races.

Passing the picturesque Murchison Cataracts he visited the powerful tribe of the Makololo, welded together by native followers of Livingstone and lately ruled over by a powerful chief, whose death in 1887 was deeply regretted. The Makololo, always friendly to the English, a fine, independent race, capable of work, open to civilisation, and competent for self-defence, had invariably been able to keep out both the Arabs and the Portuguese. On the west of Lake Nyasa, and a little inland, were situated the great tribe of the Angoni,—a race of Zulu origin, men of imposing stature, warlike, brave, and hitherto strong enough to hold their own against any Arabs opposing them. Northwards, a different, and, in some respects, a higher type of race, was found. Their huts were large and well built, with some attempt at ornament and painting; their streets, or rather the paths between the huts, were clean, and swept out every morning; their gardens skilfully cultivated, and their numerous cattle most attentively cared for. This tribe, or perhaps series of tribes of one origin and one language, the

Wa-Nkonde and the Wam-Wamba, occupy the extreme northwest and northern shores of Lake Nyasa, a lovely and most fertile plain reaching up into the hills which divide Nyasa from Tanganyika. These were the finest people seen, happy, contented, industrious, peace-loving, with qualities which could easily be developed. There is every probability that the Makololo, the Angoni, the Wam-Wamba, and minor · tribes in these territories might in the course of a few years with tact and judgment be united into one powerful nation and, guided by Englishmen, whom they are anxious to have settled amongst them, they would maintain their independence, and so form a decisive check upon the operation of the slave-trader.

Where the missionary, as may be supposed, has not made a settlement the children of the natives exposed to Arab invaders suffer dreadfully from deeds of oppression and slavery. Writing from Karonga, in 1889, Dr. Kerr Cross describes seeing a small caravan of slaves in that district which consisted merely of five boys and two girls. The day's march was over, and they sat on the ground; but the "goree-stick" was still on their neck. The leaders of the caravan were greatly perturbed at the doctor's presence and denounced him vehemently. Of the captives said the doctor, " Poor things, I pitied them with all my heart, and when I saw their upturned eyes and mangled hands and bruised, skinny bodies, and heard the white-robed ruffian talk loudly of 'his property,' I felt desperately inclined to break his head. I was enabled to rule my anger, I am glad to say. Next morning the same caravan came a few miles off their way, that they might march past our house and defy us to touch them. Surely Ethiopia, in scenes such as these, pleads for help, and stretches out her hands to God and to us against the Arab and his guns."

Another letter from Ukukwi of later date, depicts more of this nefarious work by the villainous Merere, chief of a large Arab country, and his accomplices, two Arab bands, on Mwasyoghi, a country lying at the foot of a giant hill, Rungwe, to the extreme north of the Livingstone Range. The inoffensive natives in one of the villages scarcely awakened, tried to defend themselves and to save their wives and children. So heavy was the murderous fire of the Arab guns upon them that they were driven back, and finally routed from their homesteads. A number of neighbouring villages were sacked and fired, the inhabitants of which were either killed, chained, or obliged to fly to the hills, and upwards of thirty women, with their babies, and several young girls captured. The miscreants securely entrenching themselves in a stockade of bamboos and banana-stems, settled down to enjoy themselves in their own brutish way, gorging themselves on the spoil, and glutting their savage lust by outraging the women and young girls. Disturbed in the midst of these fiendish perpetrations by some children weeping over the mutilated bodies of their mothers, certain of the inhuman wretches " unable to quiet the bairns clubbed some, and cast others into the flames of the burning houses. This is the Arab in Africa! Oh, God, raise up friends for this poor, bleeding, unhappy land! "

At Kopakopa's village, in the middle of 1889,

might have been seen five women and five children stolen from their own village with the slave-sticks on their necks. During the night the end of the sticks—young trees—were tied to the roofs of the houses, attached to which the captives lay through the chilly nights, the possible prey of hyenas or other animals. In the day-time, until sold or slain, they were allowed to crawl about the fronts of the houses always dragging the tree behind. That same year in August, Dr. Cross says : " The other day, some of our men, returning from Ukanga on the south, came across the body of a child lately thrown to the crocodiles. It was the old story. The captive mother was swooning under the load of the 'goree-stick' and her infant, when her capturer seized the child and threw it into the stream."

In sweet contrast to these dark tragedies, writes this earnest missionary at the termination of the struggle with the Arabs on the Nyasa-Tanganyika plateau : " Notwithstanding all that is disadvantageous, I have a most interesting little school held every forenoon under the trees outside the stockade. There are 300 names on the roll, with 250 in attendance. There are six classes, each taught under six giant Misyungute trees, and the children are advancing. All my little scholars at the school are children from the Wankonde villages—the very children that the Arabs fought for and longed to enslave. They are every one of them naked and helpless. God has rescued them from the slaver's cruel hand, and they look to us. Could not the children of the Sabbath-schools at home do a little for the 300 naked, helpless Wankonde children whom we have graciously saved from the cruel goree-stick and slavery?"

The schools dotting the west coast of Lake Nyasa, in 1892, are the brightest spots in the land, and where school-buildings have not yet been erected, the work is usually done in the open air, beneath the shade of a big tree, when one can be found. Lessons are taught in reading, writing, arithmetic, and Bible instruction. The fathers and mothers unable to read themselves, cannot help their children, and, not infrequently, some of them think that their chil dren should be paid for attending the school. African children in the strongly-defended villages have all kinds of ingenious amusements, of which Dr. Laws has sent details. The boys' chief game is with an india-rubber ball, in which they take two sides, and try to keep the ball always to their own party. Another game is played with beans or small stones put in hollow cups scraped out of the ground, and a curious one consists of two rows of boys sitting opposite to each other on the ground. Each of the boys sets up a little stick before him, which his companion over against it tries to knock down with little bits of calabash put on a pivot, by making them spin across at it. The boy picking up these tries in the same way to knock down the other boy's peg. The girls amuse themselves chiefly by imitating their mothers pounding grain and grinding meal and sifting it, or sometimes the little ones may be seen with a piece of cassava-root or sweet potato tied on their backs, as their mothers carry their babies.

Under the Free Church Mission flag, mission-

aries in whose breasts burns the fire of action
are serving. In 1891, Dr. Kerr Cross returned
from his home-furlough with his bride—a
step-daughter of the late Dr. Turner, the famous
South Sea missionary—for his station in North
Nyasa-land. His gentle bearing, modesty, sil-
very-toned utterance, and refined features are
unsuggestive of one who has exhibited the
most chivalrous gallantry in ministering to a
handful of men defending themselves against
overwhelming bands of Arabs. In this fight
for existence and the humanity of the slave at
Karonga's, Dr. Kerr Cross, the faithful physi-
cian, will ever be associated with Captain
Lugard and his brave garrison. Other splendid
representatives in Livingstonia who are speeding the course of missionary empire embrace Dr.
Elmslie, the translator of a primer in the language of the war-loving 'Ngoni; Dr. Henry,
of South 'Ngoni; and the Rev. A. C. Murray,
of the West Nyasa Highlands. To these add
the name, greatly revered, of the late youthful
Rev. J. Alex. Bain, whose task of love, beginning in 1883 at the most northerly outpost of

Lake Nyasa, was continued with fervid consecration and unceasing hardships until death
called him home from the sunny shores of
Bandawè on the 16th of May, 1889.

Through the formation of the African Lakes
Company, in 1878, for the development of the
country's resources and materially reinforcing
the cause of missions, a staunch ally was obtained. In a remarkable measure the missionaries have been indebted to the generous sympathy and sagacious counsels of the Livingstonia Committee at home, of which Mr. J.
Stevenson, of "Stevenson Road" fame, and
Mr. J. Campbell White, are known columns of
strength. The latter gentleman is inviting
Scotchmen to raise £20,000, to cover the fifth
period of five years, in order that the work of
the Livingstonia Mission may be consolidated
and extended.

Of the outlook over Nyasa-land there is a
broadening sunrise. Mission and civilising
agencies are progressing. Strangers unarmed
are growingly trusted by the natives, and beneath the banner of the united white influence

the tribes are peaceably disposed. Outside
these protected oases of civilisation slave-raiding has its bloody and devastating triumphs.
Against the chiefs engaged in this iniquitous
traffic Commissioner Johnston has been waging
a military crusade, and, throughout the British
Protectorate of Nyasa-land his attacks on the
Arabs, though attended by loss to his own
forces, were partially victorious at the close of
1891 and early in 1892. The anticipated future successes of this gallant officer throw a
hopeful light upon the destiny of Lake Nyasa.

In advancing the civilisation of Nyasa-land,
" customs " are being established, and postal
regulations facilitated. Land is eagerly pur-
chased, giving an impetus to agricultural prospects. That the health of Europeans can be
guaranteed is demonstrated by the sixteen
years' experience of settlers on Central African
uplands. So welcome a piece of intelligence
does not materially affect the opinion of African experts that Africa can only be cultivated,
on a broad scale, by her own people. In this
direction native labour is being employed and

the natives induced to live on the plantations. As regards entrance to the lake region it is stated that a direct passage can be made from the Indian Ocean, via the Zambesi and Shiré Rivers, as far as the foot of the Murchison Cataracts.

Dr. Kerr Cross tells a romantic story of the introduction of the coffee-plant into Nyasa-land. By way of experiment the curators of Kew Gardens sent out to Blantyre about ten years ago a number of slips of the coffee-plant. One of these alone survived the long journey and happily, it was of hardy growth. The plant took kindly to the soil, grew, bore seed, proved itself wonderfully prolific, and to-day is the progenitor of a million of plants growing on a single estate, besides hundreds of thousands on neighbouring lands. The coffee produced realises a good profit in the London market. As Dr. Cross says: "That little cutting from Kew bids fair to have a mighty civilising influence on this part of Africa, and to confer an inestimable boon on its people."

The tribes around Nyasa are a thoroughly

interesting race of people; skilful in a variety
of native trades and willing to adopt Western
ideas and handicrafts. Similar to their kins-
men on Afric's shores they yield to superstitions, depraved beliefs, witchcraft, and savage
passions. Most dreaded of their foes is the
Arab raider, in whose scorched tracks weak
and solitary tribes are marched off in chains,
" with a gun in front and one behind," or
slaughtered, which gives a world of pathos to
the observation that the African has been the
prey of the slaver ever since the dynasties of
the Pharaohs and is the blood-chattel of the
slaver to-day. Scorned by multitudes better
stationed, the dark negro ruthlessly persecuted
by woes, misfortunes, and servitude, unhelped
for ages, was more sinned against than sinning,
and with all his barbarous habits, idolatries, and
ugliness, he was a man, crying from end to end
of Africa for his heaven-born rights.

For the salvation of these lost ones the missionaries of the Eternal King have penetrated
the wildest regions and, from the dense forest
banks of the Ruo River, over the Shiré pla-

teaus, by the silvery beach of Lake Nyasa, up the Stevenson Road, across the waters of Tanganyika, and forward to the boundaries of the Congo Free State, they speak of the peace of faith, the joy of hope, and, of the life everlasting.

IN THE EMPIRE OF THE MOORS.

II.

IN THE EMPIRE OF THE MOORS.

FOR a picture of a nation's decay, corruption, darkness, and oppression, Morocco has an unhappy reputation. By missionaries and travellers alike the moral condition of the people is pourtrayed in sombre hues; a consequence partly due to bad government which in turn reflects in some measure the lawless habits of the native tribes. The wretched system of administration, —low and even declining, and universally exposed to abuse and imposition,—is vastly inferior to the Mohammedan rule exercised two centuries ago. Judged by a fair European standard government in Morocco has only a shadow of existence. The Sultan, Muley Hassan, has neither absolute power nor entire responsibility over his dominions. He is a despot of limited authority. Spending much of his time in the harem or, travelling between his two chief cities—Mo-

rocco and Fez, some three hundred miles apart
—the Sultan is content with the homage of
sovereignty and a sufficient income for his
pleasure, station, court, and pageants. The
control of Morocco is practically in the hands
of Kaids, governors of the three and thirty districts into which the empire is partitioned.
Their sway, characteristic of Eastern nations,
is marked by cruelties and extortions on an
infamous scale. The officials according to
their rank fleece the natives, and infrequently
does a superior interfere. Myriads of acres of
fine tracts of soil lie in "flat idleness" on account of the burdens imposed by tax-gatherers.
This lamentable condition of things results in
multitudes of the people existing in squalor
and destitution, and it is not surprising that in
every department of life retrogression is seen
or, that Morocco is a couple of thousand years
to the rear of the civilisation of Great Britain
and America.

Morocco—the land of song, renown, and
classic beauty—has, for ages been strangely
neglected by the civilised world. To an un-

usual degree Europe is unacquainted with it notwithstanding that about five thousand volumes describe the country's principal features and that of these books of travel, three hundred are written in the English language. The descendants of the Moors, who, for centuries, conquered and governed Spain, retain their ancestors' spirit of independence, courage, glint of refinement, and martial bearing. To kindness they are responsive and generally willing to give hospitality to strangers. The violence of character which they occasionally display is an inevitable consequence of the ill-usage and persecution inflicted upon them by the official classes. To a less extent does the degraded morality belong to the Jews in Morocco than to the Moors. In Tangier the former are influential, thrifty, enterprising, and the most enlightened part of the population, although in the adjoining provinces many of their race are the victims of gross oppression due to their alleged usurious habits. The Jews are regarded the hope of the Barbary States. In the education of the children of Morocco

Jews the present schools, few in number, are rendering a distinct service to the advance of the country, and one of the chief blessings which Christian nations could bestow on a backward and imperfectly civilised people would be, the increase of these helpful institutions. Of the mineral wealth and fertility of the land glowing accounts corroborate each other. In 1892 it was stated that maize, after paying the high rate of 105 per cent. duty, was exported in large quantities. Trade with Great Britain was considerable, and growing, and, were the Sultan not suspicious of the intrigues of foreign powers and his courtiers guilty of hiring fanatical Mohammedans in order to work on the religious fears of their co-religionists with the result of almost constant friction and ill-feeling, commercial advantages might be extended both as regards the development of native resources and the importation of manufactured articles.

Geographically viewed Morocco, "the China of the West," occupies the north-western corner of the African Continent, bounded on the

north by the Mediterranean Sea, on the east by
Algeria and the Sahara, on the south by the
giant snow-clad ranges of the Atlas Mountains,
and westwards by the blue waters of the mighty
Atlantic Ocean. The area, equal in size to five
times that of England, is about 260,000 square
miles and, on a part of its coast line, a 1,000
miles in extent, the trading settlement of Cape
Juby, Northwest Africa, is the only civilising
influence. Its population (in the absence of
official records) is estimated at from 5,000,000
to 8,000,000, consisting of Jew, Moslem, Negro,
and European. The fierce semi-independent
hill tribes governed by their own chiefs pay
scanty respect to the Sultan whose skill is displayed in keeping them in a state of perpetual
warfare to avoid revolution at home. Sultan
Muley Hassan has a "standing army" numbering 15,000 soldiers. The generalissimo of the
forces is a Scotchman bearing the title of Kaid
MacLean, who has the assistance of his brother,
both of whom were formerly officers in the British army. A description of the native warriors
presents some "rather ludicrous" aspects.

" The troops are clad in cast-off British red-coats worn not as tunics, for a Moor could never bear to be strapped up, but as loose jackets with a single button at the throat. When near enough you can see the marks of the old regimental numbers, or brigade initials, on the shoulder-pieces. A tarboosh or peaked head-piece, a pair of wide pantaloons of white, or dubious coloured cotton cloth, and the orthodox Moorish slippers, with an obsolete British musket and bayonet, completes the warrior's outfit. The British bugle-calls sound at morning, noon, and night in camp and barracks, and the words of command for military movements are given in English." A number of the soldiers and a great body of attendants join the Court on its annual progress through the provinces, an event which the natives on the line of route have reason to fear and dread. The pastoral resources of the people are usually exhausted by the demands which the Sultan's escort imposes upon these defenceless subjects. More terrible are the visits which the troops of the Sultan make in order to avenge insurrections. A large army is ordered into the district disaffected and the country for miles round is laid waste by fire and, the wretched inhabitants slaughtered in considerable numbers. In this kind of "justice," much of his Majesty's time is said to be occupied.

Slavery is quite common in Morocco. At regular intervals slave caravans arrive from Timbuctoo and the Soudan and freely distribute their " commerce." Three days a week generally in Fez, Morocco City, and other places, slave auctions are held in the open market regardless of European opinion and condemnation. This degrading traffic is an index of the social condition existing in Morocco. In the coast towns the British Minister, Sir John Drummond Hay, reports that the prohibition of the public sale of slaves has lately been infringed, a backward step greatly to be deplored. Mr. Donald MacKenzie returning from his travels in Morocco at the beginning of 1892, states that slave-dealing there is as active as ever. It is carried on more privately in the port towns, from fear of attracting the attention of the Anti-Slavery Society, but, in the interior, slaves are exposed in the public markets. A little time back the Moorish Kaids gave the Sultan and his son a present of 200 male and female slaves, to celebrate the event of the marriage of the heir to the Moorish throne. Girls, from 10 to 13 years of age, fetch about £16 to £24 each, and the slave merchants find the females more profitable from 10 to 20 years of age. Shortly before his death the lamented Sir William Kirby Green obtained a verbal promise from the Sultan that the open slave markets in his dominions should be closed,—an agreement, unfortunately, not ratified. By the new Minister at Morocco, Sir Charles Euan-Smith, active opposition to slave-selling is expected. Sir Charles's efforts on behalf of the freedom of the slave at Zanzibar are a guarantee that in Morocco he will show at the earliest opportunity his aversion to the cruel trade and, as zealously work for its stoppage.

On the unreclaimed field of Morocco the North Africa Mission and the South Morocco Mission,—the principal societies with operations,—are doing effective service. The former has twenty ladies and seven gentlemen engaged in evangelistic and similar labours at Tangier, Tetuan, Fez, and Casa Blanca, chiefly in the northern provinces. Since the opening of this mission in 1884 suitable premises have been erected and increasing influence gained over the Moslem, Jewish, Negro, and European populations.

The city of Tangier, on the north-western coast of Morocco, is the headquarters of the North Africa Mission and, the popular seaport of the missionaries. At Hope House on the city's outskirts the missionaries reside until they are accustomed to the climate and make acquaintance with Arabic. From the rocky coast which blooms with scarlet geraniums, yellow cistus, and many lovely flowers, outward and homeward bound steamers viâ the Straits of Gibraltar can easily be seen. The Tulloch Memorial Hospital at Tangier, built in memory of Miss Tulloch, a beloved labourer, and standing on the spot where she " fell asleep," is an invaluable institution, over which Dr. T.

G. Churcher exercises a capable medical and spiritual superintendence. Patients of every race and colour throng the waiting-rooms from districts where small-pox makes its ravages on Arab children, elephantiasis on adults, and, leprosy, amid Negro communities. In one of his vivid portraitures the doctor refers to a poor, sick slave from Mequinez, Central Morocco, whose face was radiant with joy at the news that the very Son of God died to save even him. Of the missionaries' highest responsibility, writes Dr. Churcher, "All our practical work is as nothing, and less than nothing, as compared with the value of one soul." The staff in Tangier includes fourteen missionaries, of which Mr. H. N. Patrick, a Spaniard, is ardently spreading the seed of the kingdom among the 4,000 Spanish in the city. Strange receptions are given to the lady missionaries. Upon a few of them visiting the market-place of Soke Hermees, in the vicinity of Tangier, every eye was fixed on them, followed with the cry, "The Nazarenes are here, the Nazarenes have come." Elsewhere the missionaries have been styled the "Nazaras" and "Kafirs,"—meaning, Infidels. Tetuan, lying on the northern skirt of Morocco, is a centre of trade and political influence. Nestling between two ranges of mountains overlooking the Mediterranean, the city has been likened in the sunshine to a "huge pearl in verdant setting." Although the population of 30,000, comprising Moslems and Jews and a sprinkling of Spaniards, has many of the leading Morocco families, its filth and crumbling ruins are typical of the polluted moral atmosphere. The city's charming natural scenery is shadowed by Mohammedan darkness, for the penetration of which serene faith has been required. As the terminus of a network of routes from the interior, Tetuan is an excellent base for missionary propagation. It forms the gateway of the Riff country which extends to Algeria. The Riff tribes, not unlike the Algerian Kabyles, are Berbers, estimated to be 200,000 in number, who show indifferent regard for the Sultan's edicts.

Fez, the Moorish capital, 130 miles from

Tangier, has 150,000 inhabitants. When Miss Herdman, its first lady missionary, was approaching it by the Sebou River, a determined Arab female seized her by the throat with one hand, and, drawing the other across it in imitation of cutting it, savagely cried out, " That is what we ought to do with you." In Fez, after seven years' toil, Miss Herdman remains, a warmly esteemed messenger of peace. Of picturesque situation rising from a circular depression, Fez is surrounded by snow-crowned summits of the higher Atlas range. The under slopes of these are clothed with orange and lemon gardens, red-leaved pomegranates, extensive olive plantations, and perennial, green shrubbery. Amid patches of golden wheat and barley, the brilliant poppies, marigolds, and groups of tinted flowers, make bright scenes. For centuries the Mogreb from the elegant tower of the historic Muley Idrees mosque has daily sounded, and, to it, the muezzins on distant minarets have as faithfully answered. In the assault on this stronghold of the False Prophet, Christ's angels of mercy have hazarded their lives, and, in the gorgeous sunsets, have climbed the flat roofs of the houses to the '*alliyahs*, to sing the melodies of Zion, or read the "Wordless Book," in the hearing of richly attired Moorish ladies and timid negress slaves. Not the least triumph of the North Africa Mission is the willingness of the Arabs to allow their wives and daughters to visit, unescorted, the mission gatherings. The medical mission at Fez is an incessantly besieged refuge in which suffering humanity is relieved. Women from towns and far-away villages assemble at the teachers' doors, and even slaves listen to the truth which maketh free indeed. One of the visitors two years ago was a black slave who, accompanying her mistress, said with glee, "I have brought her to hear about Sidna Aissa,"—the name by which Christ is known. The centre of a vast outlying population, Fez has a few dauntless pioneers and witnesses within its gates.

Since 1888 the southerly parts of Morocco have had the unswerving devotion of the missionaries belonging to the South Morocco Mis-

sion. Visiting the land in search of health, Mr.
John Anderson, of Ardrossan, was appalled at
the dark-souled condition of the people and, on
his return to Scotland, founded and, has subsequently guided, the mission, which is a
growingly powerful agency. With upwards of
twenty missionaries the mission is represented
at Rabat, Mazagan, Mogador, and Morocco City.
Unconnected with any branch of the Christian
Church the missionaries of this organization
seek to spread the kingdom of God in a plain
and unfettered manner, in harmony with Gospel teaching. The poor are visited, the young
instructed, the sick healed, and the Words of
Christ everywhere spoken in "a land of darkness, as darkness itself."

In South Morocco the state of agriculture,
communication, sanitary matters, and degradation, can hardly be conceived. Agricultural
operations remain in a crude and childish stage.
Ploughing is carried out under amusing conditions. It is a common occurrence to see
yoked together in pairs to the plough, "a pair
of bulls, a bull and a cow, a bull and a donkey,

a horse and a camel, and, a camel and a cow." When the furrows are made, or scratched, the animals stand at the ends of the plots till the Morocco peasant sows his ridges. In the far south of Morocco the Atlas Mountains supply rushing streams which are utilised for irrigation by means of the artificial water courses. Where the inhabitants have the skill and resources to make these deep channels, admirable crops are raised, once or twice annually, and the fertility of the soil increased. Fair landscapes appear on the horizon, rich in olive trees and adorned with that crown of Oriental vegetation—the picturesque date palm, welcomely availed of by travellers for shade in the neighbourhood of wells and flowing rivulets. Means of transit are of a primitive type, accomplished by mules. These animals and their masters are equally expert in protracting the time of a journey.

Mogador, on the coast, 125 miles from Morocco, is peopled chiefly by the Moors and Jews. The Mellah, the quarter in which Jews are packed, is the abode of foul smells, raging fevers, and loathsome sights, principally consequent upon the absence of drainage. Christian work in Mogador among the Jews is as burdensome as it is perilous. Much preferable is the labour of Moorish evangelisation, this race being more cleanly in habit and less crowded together than their degraded neighbours. Travelling from Mogador to Morocco, a journey which occupies five days on muleback, the country on approaching Morocco presents lovely views. A missionary traveller writes : " Passing over a fine stretch of land thickly studded with date palms, many of them laden with golden fruit, the city came in sight. Its white-washed walls and battlemented houses, and its many minarets, some of them very high, gleamed in the bright sunlight, while beyond rose the Atlas Mountains in rugged grandeur reflecting the sunshine in many brilliant hues from their snow-capped peaks and lofty slopes. The scene was one of surpassing loveliness, but its beauty only served to heighten the effect of the startling contrast within the walls of the city. The superabounding filth, the unwholesome effluvia, the perpetual discomfort, make it a most undesirable residence; while the intense and, to the European, almost unbearable stifling heat of summer, will prove no ordinary strain to physical endurance—and health." Mr. Joseph Thomson says that one-half of the population is usually in prison,—a revelation which has a pitiful climax in the spiritual blindness of the people where Moslem fanaticism flaunts itself and, on every hand, moral pollution obtains.

The subjects of the Empire of Morocco are proud, superstitious, bigoted, easily lending themselves to hatred and strife. Tens of thousands of the inhabitants in the wildest districts believe in the return of Mahomet's sway, and confidently await the hour of a mighty rising for the re-establishment of his fallen sceptre. In readiness they hold themselves for the blast of the trumpet calling them to a Holy War when, marshalled by the Sultan, they anticipate that a crushing blow will be delivered to the infidel world. Animated by this vision the natives inscribe on the guns, which they always carry, " Cineeat el jehad, in sha Allah," signifying, "For the purpose of the Holy War, if God will."

As valiantly the enthusiastic advocates of the Gospel challenge these errors and assail the frowning ramparts of Islam's power. Undis-mayed by millions of opposing Mohammedans they are assured of the presence of the Most High who prepares His own royal way, and crowns with praise and triumph the footsteps of His messengers.

LIFE PICTURES FROM NORTH AFRICAN LANDS.

(55)

III.

LIFE PICTURES FROM NORTH AFRI-CAN LANDS.

THE Arabs of North Africa cling to the style of dress and adopt the modes of etiquette by which their ancestors were known in bygone centuries. In the homestead the Arab wears his turbaned head-dress. Its removal there would be regarded a gravely discourteous act. He is accustomed to clothe himself during the winter months in a thick woollen cloak of soft drab usually some fifteen feet long, which almost completely swathes his hardy limbs. With a portion of the shawl he makes his turban and, another length he ties up to serve as a purse. A smartly contrived red leather pocket hangs at the side suspended by shoulder-straps in addition to a broad, richly-dyed, cloth girdle round the waist, forming a great support in the trying changes of heat and

cold, peculiar to the African climate. The
yellowish-brown sandals worn in travelling over
thorny or stony ground are generally ex-
changed on approaching a dwelling, for a pair
of shoes, with the heels turned in, which make
it easier to remove them on entering a tent or
room.   In this artistic costume the Arab has
a picturesqueness of figure which breathes of
the " billowy," sandy desert.

For the exquisite growths of nature the
Arabs, men and women alike, have scanty
regard.   The brightest-hued flowers are care-
lessly passed.   About the doorways of " gour-
bis," or, on the roofs of better-class dwellings,
mint for tea, oranges for eating, and a little
coriander and parsley, with which to flavour
dishes of soup, are cultivated, and this is their
ideal of a garden.   A missionary correspondent
thus sketches a winter garden at Fez, in December: " We were in a beautiful garden full
of orange, lemon, and other fruit trees, with
rose and white jasmine bushes in bloom.   The
oranges are still sour, but the trees, full of yellow fruit with their dark glossy leaves, are

always a pleasing picture. The Moorish idea
of a garden is *produce.* The flowers are only
allowed odd corners where there is no room for
a tree, or close to the narrow paths of beaten
earth. Jasmine and roses pulled off without
stems are saleable, the jasmine to make
wreaths for the ladies' heads, the roses for
rosewater. The blossom of the bitter orange
is sold in large quantities in the spring for dis-
tillation." In the spring-time it is quite a
pleasant novelty to meet an Arab girl who has
a sprig of jasmine or a violet in her hair. If a
flower is to interest them it must have the essential quality of sweetness; the cultivation of
anything *just to admire,* is entirely beyond
their idea. And so it has been noticed that
when Europeans introduce flowers for delight
only, the Arabs are always surprised and re-
quire training in order to appreciate the charms
of floral beauty. In this respect they offer a
distinct contrast to their not far off Andalusian
neighbours in such a city as Seville. Of the
women employed there in one of the tobacco
factories a visitor recently made this observa-

tion : " One womanly trait was almost universal, the love of flowers. The ugliest slat-
tern, equally with the comparatively neat woman, had a flower or two in her hair, on her
bosom, or in a jug beside her table. It was a
little bit of pure nature in a very dark and de-
pressing human dungeon."

In all the North African regions women have
a thankless life. They are generally penned
up in what may be termed prison houses or
made to labour in the most degrading fashion.
From very early childhood hundreds of women,
for instance, in Tunisian villages, never leave
their cheerless, shabby homes, not even to go
to a public bath, which a few of their more
favoured sex can enjoy. Necessarily these
poor creatures are of a sad and forlorn type,
and so enslaved to traditions that upon a European entering their domicile they promptly
close the door behind him to avoid the risk of
a man happening to pass at the time, an occurrence which is supposed to bring disgrace on
the females within. A lady missionary in
Tunis touchingly depicts the condition of Arab

females: "Only a woman! a poor, worn-out, broken-hearted woman—old before her time—in the eyes of her Mohammedan husband, a slave, married to be the mother of his children, a part of his possessions, to be cast off at his pleasure, to be shut up from year's end to year's end with very little change to break the dull monotony of her life : only a household drudge !
. . . . Do you want to know the truth of this? There are countries, not a week's journey from England, where our sisters are treated like beasts rather than women—left without education, shut in, married one day, divorced the next ; living loveless lives, without any present Saviour, only a dim, false hope in the future, but oh ! so willing to learn and listen, if only they are reached in time."

Among Algerian tribes women are forced to do the hardest kinds of labour outside the tents. They gather and carry piles of wood long distances, draw the water for the household, make the rude pottery, take charge of the flocks, and regularly milk the cows and goats. These burden-bearers weave the men's haiks, and, with deft hands work the mats and baskets which are offered for sale. The poorer classes are seldom clean in person. Those who have lost sons or male relations in war must not wash or change their garment, made up of several yards of calico or muslin fastened with wooden pins. A missionary trying to persuade a young woman to wash her baby and his garment, as it was nothing but dirt that was killing the child, received the reply, " Has there not died to us enough of our men in the war that I should let him die also?" Their houses are barely worthy the name, so meanly are they furnished and lacking in cleanliness.

From a sense of fear the Arabs, as a rule, in every part of North Africa, sleep together, and alongside them may be, a camel, mule, cow and calf, goat, pig, or a half-starved dog or cat. In the remote, less civilised districts of Southern Algeria, the women put off the face veil, a portion of attire which among women of beauty and those of the upper classes in the northerly towns is rigidly worn, save over a part of the left eye. The Kabyle women, whose race in thousands occupy a large division of Northern Algeria, are more kindly treated than any other section of females in North Africa. Unlike the nomadic Arabs, the Kabyles are settled, home-loving tribes of people. In spite of their darkened lives their taste and orderliness are noticed in the well-tilled farms and fruitful market gardens, nor are the women veiled after the custom of their Arab neighbours. One of the interesting adornments of a woman in Kabylia is a brooch attached to her forehead, which denotes that she has had the distinction of bearing a son, and as frequently as the honour is repeated, she adds to the number of her ornaments with true native grace and dignity.

Curiosity and suspicion are universal traits. When a stranger is invited into an Arab tent, and has put off his shoes before stepping on the mat, the eagerness to learn everything about him is astonishing. Of this character-istic, laughable stories are told by the ladies of the North Africa Mission. In certain parts where a foreign lady may not have previously travelled, her dress is an object of minute and

incessant examination. The natives are amazed
at the quantity of flannel worn by Europeans.
Hats, too, are respectfully inspected and the
under-garments scrutinized by the native women, who wear little beside two or three cotton folds. When this inspection is finished,
questioning begins regarding the life-history of
the guest. As with Easterns of other lands, the
Arabs are painfully suspicious, a feature of a
less pleasing character. Deceiving and deceived, they are loth to commit themselves to
a fresh face, and much effort is required to persuade them of genuine friendliness. When
their confidence is gained the kindness they
show in the north country provinces is remarkable. A friend of the writer's recently travelled on foot from Tunis to Gabes, a fortnight's
journey, upwards of two hundred miles, without the slightest charge for hospitality, except
on one occasion. On money being offered to
the Bedouin Arabs for shelter and refresh-
ments they often replied in their own tongue:
"The Lord has given me plenty, I don't want
your money."

Pathetic to the last degree is the death scene on many a stern landscape among the Bedouin children of the desert. When the dread hour approaches the suffering member usually rests on a mattress in the middle of the floor. From far and near friends and relatives slide in to watch, until the apartment is unbearably crowded. The appearance of these death-watchers is very strange and uncivilised. Their hair jet black, their faces painted, and, their clothing, made up of loose, dark blue garments, is thrown up on the shoulder or across the chest, fastened by a huge pin adorned with a large silver ring. There they remain hour after hour and only turn away when life has ceased to beat. In their customs the Bedouins differ little from the stationary Arabs : they are Mohammedans, densely igno-rant, superstitious in the extreme, yet more accessible by Europeans.

That useful adjunct of civilised lands, the post-carrier, has a rough kind of existence in North Africa. The only " royal mail " in Mo-rocco is represented by a class of poor, lean

Arabs, bearing letters in leathern bags slung about their necks. A traveller pourtrays the type of present-day Moorish post-runners: " They eat nothing on their journey but a little bread and a few figs ; they stop only at night for a few hours to sleep, with a cord tied to the foot, to which they set fire before going to sleep, and which wakens them within a certain time ; they travel whole days without seeing a tree or a drop of water ; they cross forests infested with wild boar, climb mountains inaccessible to mules, swim rivers, sometimes walk, sometimes run, sometimes roll down declivities, or climb ascents on feet and hands, under the August sun, under the drenching autumn rains, under the burning desert wind, taking four days from Fez to Tangier, a week from Tangier to Morocco, from one extremity of the empire to the other, alone, barefooted, half-naked ; and when they do reach their journey's end, they go back ! And this they do for a few francs." Than the lives of these couriers nothing more wretched can be imagined.

At the elementary steps towards civilisation the Arabs and Bedouins look on very stubbornly in the myriad villages of the French Regency in Tunis. Near to the hamlet dwellings of the natives stagnant water, heaps of filthy mire, and the bodies of decayed animals foul the atmosphere and, as of yore, spread horrible diseases. When the inhabitants are urged to remove these vile sources of pestilence opposite their hovels, in which the sick are lying, they invariably answer: " We have always been accustomed to leave them unburied." The cramped, irregular, misnamed streets are used for cooking, trading, shambles, and, not infrequently, to suit the native humour of the population, grotesque theatrical displays. Morality in such quarters is rarely found. Untruthfulness, dishonesty, and treachery prevail, nor have the people much affection for each other.

Tunis, the capital of the province, is a city of faded glory, vice, and degradation, of some 140,000 inhabitants. These are made up of 30,000 Jews, 20,000 to 30,000 Italians, French,

Arabs, Berbers, and Maltese. The city, five miles in circumference, has an outer wall of nine gates, enclosing an inner one, which has seven smaller entrances. Famed for its magnificent mosque and teeming with mosques of miniature size, Tunis was built in an age when the mighty Ottoman empire stood in the zenith of its power and renown. The Oriental character of the streets make a kaleidoscopic panorama, garnished with bazaars in the arched, fretted arcades, and trodden by the world's nationalities, through which strings of soft-footed camels, caparisoned mules, and donkeys jostle and struggle for passage. Arab women of rank travel secluded in closed carriages accompanied by negresses of the better type veiled or masked in black, with the exception of a narrow slit through which they gaze on the busy scene. The city is dead to spiritual life and its drunkenness is appalling. One missionary says: "The greatest hindrance to missionary progress here is alcohol. Friends who think that the Mohammedans are sober people ought to come and spend a week with us that

they might see the contrary." Another writes:
" The longer I live in Tunis the more I see and
hear of its awful wickedness." In this province,
one of the darkest throughout North Africa,
thousands upon thousands of blinded Moslems
piously observe the five leading injunctions of
the Koran—belief in God, and Mohammed (His
chief prophet), almsgiving, pilgrimage to Mecca,
fasting in the month of Ramadan, and prayer.
It is interesting to hear a Mohammedan add,
" if God will," whenever he is about to make a
journey, and as painful, his exclamation, " God
is great," in all kinds of stations and circumstances where, commonly, every vestige of
morality is denied. In the haunts and homes
of these people, heroines of the faith, filled with
the spirit of the Gospel, are telling of One
mighty to help and save.

Slavery is a national abomination and in-
iquity. Into Tripoli, Tunis, Algeria, and Morocco, gangs of slaves are brought continually
in vast numbers from the interior for sale.
Were the inhuman cruelties inflicted on the
hapless beings adequately known, the removal

of the villainy of slave-trading in these parts would not long be postponed. A sense of guilt is shown by the traders in the western provinces of Morocco. At Fez, the Moorish capital, the slave market is hypocritically styled, " El Soke Baraka," the " Market of Blessing," and many of the slaves bought there receive affectionate names by which slave dealers and owners try to deaden a reproaching conscience. In Morocco the slaves have one right only. If a master very brutally outrages his " chattel," the victim may seek redress from a local judge who can command the proprietor to sell his slave. Seldom is the privilege exercised by the captive, lest the second owner should prove worse than his predecessor.

Although brilliant results have not hitherto attended the North Africa Mission, its missionaries have excelled in planting Gospel seeds in Islamite furrows, in acts of Christ-like mercy, and, in beginning the foundation of the sovereign faith. The mission, inaugurated eleven years ago,—previous to which there was no evangelistic organisation occupied in the great

North African provinces,—has enrolled seventy workers, opened six Medical Missions, and initiated a group of agencies by which to reclaim some of the fourteen million souls populating the lands which skirt the curving northern shores of the Mediterranean Sea.

EVANGELISATION IN EGYPT AND THE NILE VALLEY.

IV.

EVANGELISATION IN EGYPT AND THE NILE VALLEY.

BRIGHTENING signs mark the progress of education, agriculture, and civilisation in Lower and Upper Egypt,—blessings of a social and material character which have largely flowed from the British occupation which began about seven years ago. In the work of pacific revolutionising Sir Evelyn Baring and his distinguished staff have done more in a very brief period than Egypt's rulers did in long centuries to establish justice, to raise the " fellaheen " from hereditary bondage, and to develop the untilled resources of a land

" Where all things always seem'd the same."

The régime of Turkey over Egypt, characterised too frequently by oppression and ruinous taxation, has been firmly supplanted by a rule instinct with the spirit of humanity and righteousness. Every well-wisher of this deeply interesting country will desire to see her prosperity continued under the sceptre of the new sovereign, the young Khedive, Abbas Pasha.

The growth recently, almost phenomenal, of the public school system, has signal value. It is scarcely credible that the earlier unwillingness of the natives to avail themselves of this institution is already disappearing. An illustration of this is shown in the return of 1887, when there were only 12 Government schools with 1,919 pupils, in contrast to the number of schools in 1890,—as far south as Assouan,—counted at 47, with an attendance of 7,307, and a corresponding increase in paying, as distinct from aided, scholars. The voluntary principle of the education offered makes the improvement more notable.

Passing to the sphere of evangelisation and missionary activity the palm of honour is carried off easily by the United States. The work of the American Presbyterians inaugurated seven and thirty years since has been equally remarkable in the energy displayed and the spiritual harvest obtained. Far up the Nile banks, where

"Tall Orient shrubs, and obelisks
Graven with emblems of the time,"

abound, they have laboured with unwearied ardour. Testimonies have often been given by European tourists of the religious enthusiasm of American missionaries which may cause English Christians to blush, particularly so, on recalling what British statesmanship has achieved for the material and national welfare of modern Egypt.

In Cairo—a base of Christian aggression—the celebrated Mohammedan University of El Azar is situated, to which upwards of 10,000 Moslem students resort from north and east Africa, Turkey, Arabia, Persia, and India, for the exclusive study of the Koran and its literature. Some of these return to the empires of the East to propagate Moslem doctrines, and others, in considerable numbers, attach themselves to Mohammedan leaders in the Dark Continent as crusading preachers and conquerors, thus swelling the rising tide of Mohammedanism

setting in from North African lands. As far
back as 1860, in that most Oriental-looking of
Eastern cities—Cairo, Miss Mary Whately,
whose death in March, 1890, was widely lamented, opened her British school on Christian
principles, and, later, another valuable auxiliary,—the Medical Mission. With rare self-
sacrifice this benevolent lady, one of the
daughters of Archbishop Whately, gave, in
furtherance of these objects, her entire strength
and private means. By the Khedivial Government and by every class of residents and officers in the city, these institutions were appreciated. An evidence of the usefulness of the
Medical Mission is the report that weekly,
throughout the year, more than 300 patients
had relief. The work of the late Miss M. L.
Whately has been continued by Mrs. Shakoor and
the Hon. Diana Vernon,—but in future a union
with the Church Missionary Society is probable.
Of kindred aim in Cairo is the home for freed wom-
en slaves which was instituted several years ago
by the British and Foreign Anti-Slavery Society. Dusky strangers from southern climes are

trained within the home and remain there until they are qualified to enter domestic service
or are married. A similar home has recently
been organised in the city of Tripoli, for refu-
gee slave women, by Ahmed Ressim Pasha, the
enlightened Governor-General of the province
of Tripoli,—a harbinger, it may be hoped, of
stronger opposition to the slave trade in the
surrounding countries.

The missionary occupation of Lower Egypt,
or the Delta, is painfully insufficient for the
needs of a population approaching six millions
of souls. Of the 400,000 inhabitants in Cairo
there are possibly 4,000 regular hearers of the
Gospel. The workers in 1891 comprised three
missionaries and four ladies belonging to the
English Church Missionary Society, whose labours in household visitation, in Christian
schools, and in the Medical Mission, have been
growingly fruitful. The literary and medical
departments have respectively had the able
superintendence of Drs. Klein and Harpur,
who have made a vigorous appeal to the directors in England for sixteen additional seed-

sowers to hasten Egypt's ingathering.   In the
same city the United Presbyterian Church of
North America has extensive schools and large
congregations, and, over the Delta, in five of
the principal towns and about a score of the
villages, various schools and small companies
of worshippers.   On this wide field the American Mission force is limited to the efforts of
two missionaries and four ladies, reckoning
missionaries' wives, and its staff of devoted native helpers.   The seaport of Alexandria, with
a population of 230,000 souls, has one missionary, three lady visitors to the harems, a Church
of Scotland missionary responsible for an Arab
children's primary school, two lady missionaries engaged in general services under General
Haigh's direction, Miss Robinson's much esteemed Sailors' and Soldiers' Institute, and, Mr.
Rudolph's visits to the Jews.   Other spiritual
agencies employed on the Delta include a
Dutch missionary at Calioub, near Cairo, an
occasional colporteur at Damietta, evangelists
for the Europeans and sailors at Port Said, and
the indefatigable witness-bearers of the English

and American Bible Societies who cannot expect very bright results in a land where, it is said, only four or five per cent. can read.

· Little has the extreme spiritual darkness of the Delta or, the vastness of its unoccupied territory, been realised. Excluding Cairo and Alexandria and their great populations and a number of smaller towns whose inhabitants vary from 5,000 to 40,000 each, there are thousands of mud-built villages on the brown-mounds—the remains of villages of a bygone epoch, in which millions of souls live wholly destitute of the light of the Gospel. With the advancing strides of civilisation the level stretches of the Delta, the threading canals, the broad patches of vivid green large-leafed clover (the native *berseem*), may by and by become the centres of evangelical faith. On that soil, fertile as historical, over which fifty dynasties and ten nationalities have ruled nearly seven thousand years, where generations of native races have in succession been crushed beneath the heel of Assyrian, Persian, Roman, Saracen, and Turkish satraps and despots, the prophet's vision must be fulfilled: "And the Lord shall be known to Egypt, and the Egyptians shall know the Lord in that day."

To the shadow which falls on the Delta the brightness of the day-spring which has visited the Nile Valley, south of Cairo, presents a cheering contrast. For a distance of 400 miles up the Nile which represents Egypt proper, since the Equatorial Regions and other provinces stretching from Arabia Petræa and Syria to the western limits of Darfur in Central Africa, were lost during the late Khedive's reign, the United Presbyterians of North America have honoured themselves in organising the most notable and successful mission on Egyptian territory in modern times. Along this comparatively narrow strip of alluvial soil, hemmed in by hills through which the Nile flows, fringed with green banks and the stately, graceful palms, lives a population of about 1,000,000 people, among whom the Americans have toiled with surprising devotion. On this riverine tract, covering districts as far apart as Mansoora and Luxor, El Feshn and Kench, Asyoot and

Assouan, they have ninety stations with schools attached, or congregations and schools united, taught by native pastors and teachers. As proof of the vitality of the work is the statement that the eighty and more schools are entirely supported by the willing offerings of the native congregations. With the thirty-five congregations and schools in Cairo, its environs, and the Delta, the total membership of the native evangelical churches numbers 3,200, making in 1890 a gain of seventeen and one-half per cent. Three years ago 25,944 religious meetings were held ; the average Sunday morning attendance at worship reached 4,747, and the Sunday-schools, 4,338. For the privileges of public worship and in aid of the Zenana mission, the natives are liberal contributors. In the evangelistic department the native workers consist of pastors, licentiates, Bible-readers, theological students, Zenana visitors upwards of sixty in number, together with 250 Sunday-school teachers ; and, by means of 15 colporteurs, who travel annually hundreds of miles, and numerous book depôts, 33,609 publications of an educational and religious class were sold. The section devoted to education is represented by 5,600 pupils in the Mission common schools, a training college and theological seminary for pastors and teachers, and training schools for girls which furnish teachers and Zenana workers. By the attendance of something like 1,000 Moslem boys and girls at the schools, the influence of the Mission is abundantly testified, and, as remarkably, by the baptism of sixty young men and women, formerly Mohammedans, into the Christian faith. From every social rank, grade, and tribe come the scholars to receive the advantages of an education imparted in an ennobling, Christian spirit. The girls are qualified for the domestic circles as maids or, for the position of wives in the homes ; and the boys excel as skilled artisans, if not selected for Government offices. To promote the agencies of this singularly noble undertaking, the Nile Mission boat, the *Ibis*, constantly makes voyages up and down the river, admirable buildings are being erected, and, an aggregate staff of 300 efficient co-labourers, native and foreign, engaged.

Mainly has the plough of the American missionaries been turned upon the Coptic dwellers in the Nile Valley, who form with the Mohammedans a large proportion of the population. On this fallow ground they have toiled and won bright triumphs. In a twofold sphere success has been reaped. Zealous converts have been made and, by thousands the young people have flocked into the schools. A wave of revival has reached the Coptic Church,—an ancient branch of Christendom and, not improbably, its restoration may be graciously achieved by men and women taught in the churches of the American Mission. Upon the Mohammedans the energy of the missionaries has made an impression. Less bigoted than their co-religionists westwards, they have been affected by contact with Europeans and upheavals in the history of the Soudan, and are, to-day, more susceptible to the message of Christ. The lines of the poet:

" Neither hide the ray
From those, not blind, who wait for day,"

have distinct application to these followers of
the False Prophet, from whose midst a harvest
of souls may yet be gathered.   In Egypt, " the
Egypt of the Pharaohs and the Ptolemies,"
across whose sandy deserts and gigantic ruins
the sun has poured his heat for uncounted
ages, the heralds of the Cross are setting before the eyes of the native Mohammedans, at
the close of the nineteenth century, the holi-
ness and grace of Christianity, by which to un-
bar the hearts of multitudes to the power of
salvation and the kingdom of God.

Such divine success may receive impetus
from high places.   In the new Egyptian Ministry of 1891 the two portfolios of the Foreign
Minister and the Minister of Public Instruction
were placed in the hands of native Christian
statesmen.   Tigrane Pasha, the holder of the
first named office, is young, brilliant, and, of independent mind, who, in the discharge of two
previous under-secretaryships, has shown eminent ability, and gained the reputation of being

a powerful ally. The second of these appoint-
ments is held by Yacoub Pasha Artin, who
signalised his under-secretaryship in the same
department at an earlier date by founding the
current system of education and effecting reforms of national importance. No longer will
it be possible to repeat the indignities to which
they were subjected on account of their Christian profession by Riaz Pasha, a former President of the Council, inasmuch as each of these
distinguished servants of State will have the
confidence, which they enjoyed at the hands of
the late Khedive, from his successor.

By these exalted personages it is not un-
reasonable to hope that Christianity will have
open countenance; their Mohammedan col-
leagues the influence of Christian manhood;
the destinies of Egypt the stamp of a genuinely
humane policy; and, the Eastern world, the
rays of an enlightened rule, before which "the
voice of the oppressor" shall cease and the
night of darkness forever be chased away.

UGANDA UNDER CONQUEST.

V.

UGANDA UNDER CONQUEST.

WITH a country of exceeding fertility, capable of enormous productiveness, and peopled by the finest nation in Africa, Uganda, to the north-west of Victoria Nyanza, is one of the most powerful kingdoms in East Central Africa. To reach Uganda from the coast at Zanzibar has involved forced and desperate marches attended by no slight peril. The transport of goods, confined to human porterage, and estimated at an average cost of £200 per ton, from the seaboard of the Indian Ocean to the lake region, has been unusually trying and burdensome. By this primitive mode of carriage the journey has required four months for accomplishment. To carry 250 tons a sum of £50,-000 must be paid to 1,000 men, slaves as a rule, hired out by slave-owners to do the work. Pledged to the total suppression of slavery

the British East Africa Company has utilised
this form of contract to the slave's advantage,
and upwards of 4,000 slaves have effected their
emancipation by the proceeds of transit labour.
Where necessary they have likewise secured
the protection offered in the freed slave settlements.   On the construction of the projected
railroad for which a survey is in progress the
inhuman practice of enslaving captives will
have received in the sphere of British influence
its desired overthrow : the rescue of slaves will
be more frequent, caravan routes severed, and,
a distinct beginning made towards the extermination of the life-curse which has lain for
long ages on the face of the Dark Continent.
It is calculated that the railway system, extending from the sea-coast to the Victoria Nyanza,
will measure something like 500 miles.   In
leading this admirable enterprise the British
East Africa Company,—a governing corpora-
tion engaged in the work of developing and
opening routes for British trade and the commerce of the world,—will more effectively cover
a coast line of over 400 miles and, stretching

from 8co to 1,000 miles into the interior. This extensive area is amazingly rich in natural re- sources and in its normal condition supports large herds of cattle, supplies grain in excess of the needs of its ordinary population, and, is susceptible of bearing an increased variety of agricultural produce. In contact with the mill- ions of semi-barbarians, civilisation is already creating wants, chiefly of textile manufacture, which will certainly be multiplied by the intro- duction of industries necessitating much inter- change of commodities.

The circle of missionary endeavour has no more romantic narrative than that written on the field of heathendom in Uganda. Since the month of November, 1875, when Mr. Stanley's challenge to Christendom appeared in a Lon- don newspaper, heroically brave soldiers of the Cross have waged battle for its conquest. Seven months after the call for missionaries had been made the first mission party of the English Church Missionary Society had arrived at Zanzibar, where preparations were promptly in hand for the march inland. Through what periods of light and shade their labours have passed in Uganda the world has gleaned from letters' and diaries of tragic interest. The promising opening of the mission was darkened by the murder of Lieutenant Smith and Mr. O'Neill and, two years later, the hostile influence of Arab traders and the coming of several French Romish priests prejudiced Mtesa, the king, against the English missionaries. At the close of 1879 the missionaries were shocked at the king's return to heathen customs. The following year the reduced band of evangelists quietly pursued their task of sowing the Word among the native population. By the month of March, 1881, the Uganda envoys returned from England, the storm-cloud lifted, impetus was given to the campaign, and fresh reinforcements arrived. The first converts, five in number, were baptised on the 18th of March, 1882, the reaping continuing in spite of the Monarch's doubtful attitude. In 1884, Mtesa, after a reign of twenty-seven years, died, and, one evidence of the hold which the missionaries had upon the court and chiefs, was their prevention of the barbaric cruelties which had been enacted for centuries in connexion with a sovereign's funeral obsequies.

Mwanga's accession to the throne was the beginning of a series of events of a chequered character. As the murderer of Bishop Hannington and the Christian "readers," in 1886, Mwanga's name was tarnished with a bloody memory. That calamity stirred Christendom throughout its length and breadth and evoked profound sympathy with the cause of African missions. Dark days of persecution and massacre rapidly succeeded one another, the missionaries in the meantime, Mackay, notably, suffering great hardships. From conscience or policy Mwanga, in 1888, looked with favour on the Revs. E. C. Gordon and R. H. Walker, and every hope was entertained of progress. In the same year Mwanga was dethroned by a revolution and the sceptre placed in the hands of his brother Kiwewa, who was deposed and murdered by the Arab party, and another brother, named Kilema, invested with kingly rank. This puppet of evil masters commenced his rule by slaughtering all his princely brothers and sisters, and, with one exception, Mwanga's immediate kindred. The king's deeds of blood swiftly recoiled on his own fortunes! In his banishment the exile Mwanga took refuge with the French missionaries at the south end of Victoria Nyanza, where he eagerly seconded their plans to reinstate him in Uganda. His allied fugitives associated with the French teachers next attacking Kilema in two pitched battles,—one at Uddu and another across the Katonga, in which they were victorious. Mwanga subsequently joined these assailants and after alternate defeats and successes regained the throne. It should be chronicled to the undying honour of Mr. Mackay that although he was pressingly urged when exiled at Usambiro to encourage the Protestant native converts to unite themselves with Kilema's foes, he unhesitatingly opposed the stratagem. By the death of Kilema, his predecessor reigns without a rival, nor has he any successor, save in the person of a little son, a few years old. Amid these struggles the country was in a sorry condition. An explorer who travelled through it spoke of the desolation which starvation and bloodshed had produced. This eye-witness questioned whether at the head of the kingdom " there ever was a man more unfitted to rule a country (than Mwanga), as he takes absolutely no interest in the welfare of his people, but only thinks of his own safety and personal comforts. Banana groves and several small coffee plantations were choked up with long grass and in a dreadful state of neglect. Human remains and broken shields were scattered along the path, and everything bore signs of the recent troubles."

To complete the picture of 1890 it will naturally be assumed that Mwanga was the nominee of the Catholic party. At heart he was a ruler by expediency who would have crushed both Catholics and Protestants if it had been within his power, and, on the other hand, the natives of Uganda, had they possessed a prince of Mtesa's line, would have put forward his claims. The design of the French agents to have political control in Uganda has created endless bitterness between the Protestant and Catholic converts, again inflamed in 1891–2, consequent upon the representatives of the British East Africa Company administering justice irrespective of class or tribe. The one bright spot in the train of these disasters was the treaty which Mwanga made at Mengo, May 16, 1890, with the signatories, Père Simeon Lourdel (since dead), of the Algerian Missions, and Dr. Carl Peters,—that slave dealing and the exportation of slaves from territory under his jurisdiction, should be forbidden. With Dr. Felkin's remarks on the question of the Romish invasion in Uganda most readers will be in hearty accord. He writes: "One cannot help believing that in uncivilised countries, such as Uganda, missions of various denominations should not encroach one upon the other. Probably ecclesiastics may differ on this point; still it can hardly be doubted that had the Protestants, who first entered Uganda, been permitted to carry on their work without the disruption caused by the subsequent introduction of an apparently new religion, much would have been different, and the undoubted advantages which the Protestants possessed in 1880 might have served to prevent the intrigues which led to such loss of life."

In 1890 Bishop Tucker, the third Bishop of Equatorial Africa, reached Usambiro after a rough journey. Arriving in Uganda he perceived the jealousy of the French Roman Catholic missionaries and, the uneasiness of the people, lest the Mohammedans should invade Mwanga's dominions. With the enthusiasm of the Protestant converts he was overjoyed, of which he wrote on December 30, 1890: "Truly, the half was not told me. Exaggeration about the eagerness of the people here to be taught, there has been none. No words can describe the emotion which filled my heart as on Sunday, the 28th, I stood up to speak to fully 1,000 men and women, who crowded the church of Buganda. It was a wonderful sight! There, close beside me, was the Katikiro, the second man in the kingdom. There, on every hand, were chiefs of various degrees, all Christian men, and all in their demeanour devout and earnest to a high degree. The responses in their heartiness were beyond everything I have heard even in Africa. There was a second service in the afternoon, at which there must have been fully 800 present. The same earnest attention was apparent and the same spirit of devotion. I can never be sufficiently thankful to God for the glorious privilege of being permitted to preach to these dear members of Christ's flock." The Bishop set apart in January, 1891, six natives as lay evangelists, who will be entirely supported by the native church. Hopes are cherished that shortly they may become candidates for the order of the clergy. Unlimited possibilities seem to be within the compass of the Christians of Uganda. Taught by each other it appears that numbers of the converts have never had the advantage of a white teacher, while, as pleasing, is the desire of native converts to support the ministry in their midst. The Bishop was partly successful in negotiating pledges for more amicable relations between the two divisions into which the Christians

have ranged themselves. About the middle
of 1891 Bishop Tucker made a hurried visit to
England to secure 40 volunteer missionaries,
and to hold conferences with the committee
respecting future policy in Uganda. His ad-
dresses aroused great interest in the United
Kingdom, followed by promises of large sub-
scriptions and offers of service. The tidings
of missionary progress in Uganda were confirmed later by the Rev. E. C. Gordon, on furlough from Uganda. He spoke of the influence which the Protestant chiefs and converts,
though inferior numerically to the Roman
Catholics, exerted, by their strong character
and fidelity. In their wish to learn the truth
they were most earnest and had built houses
for the missionaries and a church of considerable size. The results of the work, in every
way, were marvellous. From the Church Missionary Society's directors, Mr. Gordon had a
hearty greeting. This splendid missionary
sailed with his uncle, the martyr-bishop Hannington, at whose suggestion Cyril Gordon left
wife and friends behind in entering on the haz-

ardous " call " to the Dark Continent. Leaving
England together in 1882,—the following year,
Hannington was. driven back by fever, but
again returned in 1884 to the land he had
learned to love, as first bishop in Eastern
Equatorial Africa. At the time of Hannington's tragical fate Gordon was spared, and
through nine long years heroically toiled. One
may write of him :

" For where he fixt his heart he set his hand
  To do the thing he will'd, and bore it thro'."

Upon Gordon's vigorous constitution the climate and trials have furrowed deep marks.
His testimony shows that Mr. Stanley's tributes to Alexander Mackay's splendid labours in Uganda were not exaggerated and,
worthy of a race some of whom had refused
for Christ's sake the personal advantage of being made chieftains, and, of others, who had
endured scorching persecution, and had per-
sisted in cherishing a Christian profession at
the peril of their lives.

Zeal in England for the Uganda Mission

was tested and crowned late in 1891. The Directors of the British East Africa Company finding that their financial outlay in Uganda was heavy and without adequate return, had resolved to withdraw, a step which intensified the risk of the missionaries and their settlements. Captain Lugard, that brave man, whose tact, energy, sagacity, and resources had, in 1891, saved Uganda from being torn to pieces by internecine strife, if not devoured by coast Arabs or, the Mahdi's vedettes, was recalled. To avert this contingency the Company offered to advance a large amount of money if the Society's friends would guarantee a similar amount. Enough to add, that the supporters of the Uganda crusade grandly responded, a proof of the enthusiasm which the work in prospect and achieved in Uganda, had inspired. It would have been pitiable if this most interesting of the African tribes had been forsaken in the hour of trial when so many had attested their faith by martyrdom and others were prepared to endure hardship for the Cross.

On the eve of departure for Africa in De-

cember, 1891, Bishop Tucker appealed to Christian and philanthropic people of the United
Kingdom to enable the missionaries to place a
steel steamboat on the Victoria Nyanza, the cost
of which and her provision for two years would
amount to £25,000. Except the laying of a
railway no more potent instrument could be
utilised for the destruction of slavery and the
slave trade,—the greatest curse which afflicted
humanity in Central Africa ; than a powerful
steamer, far superior to the small steel sailing
vessel *en route* for the lake. The steamer
would serve for police purposes, the interests
of the natives, and, of civilisation generally. In
particular it would be a grand agent in extending to the regions beyond, the priceless
blessings of Christianity.

Touchingly the Bishop alluded to a conference of six men, some five years back, on
the southern shore of the Victoria Nyanza.
The topic of these heroes who had consecrated
their lives to the service of their fellow-creatures was the need of a steamer for lake navigation. They unanimously agreed that the

craft was indispensable if the work was to go forward effectively. Three of the six men, Henry Perrot Parker, the second bishop of Equatorial Africa, who presided over the conference; Henry Blackburn, and Alexander Mackay, now lie in their graves, less than 100 yards from the very spot where their conference was held. The names of the three survivors are Robert H. Walker, Robert P. Ashe, and Douglas Hooper. Mackay had himself undertaken to build the vessel and, with iron will he toiled beneath the fierce rays of an African sun for its consummation. The task was beyond the strength of this crusader of missions, who fell in the forge as nobly as any hero-warrior on the battle field. Riveting the plates of the boiler he was seized with a chill which alas, proved fatal, on the 8th of February, 1890.

It cannot be long ere the funds are subscribed for the realisation of Mackay's sacred ambition, " that marvellous dream of the Empress of Uganda, who saw a beautiful boat with white wings spread out like a great sea-bird sailing over the waters of the Nyanza with a white man seated in the stern looking at the land." On the project of such a vessel the missionary's heart was set and, for it he gave up his life. Than the erection and dispatch of this craft no grander memorial could be raised to commemorate Mackay's sacrifices on behalf of " many millions of mankind whose civilisation is perhaps the brightest realistic vision of this century." Together with comrades of heroic fortitude his dust lies on the pebbly shores of Victoria Nyanza. The services to humanity of these brave men are o'er,. they have entered into rest, and yet, in the tide of coming years, their dauntless faith will be as a living inspiration to Christian nations. These "dead, but unconquerable" witnesses have attested that:

" The path of duty was the way to glory :
He, that ever following her commands,
On with toil of heart and knees and hands,
Thro' the long gorge to the far light has won
His path upward, and prevail'd,
Shall find the toppling crags of Duty scaled
Are close upon the shining table-lands
To which our God Himself is moon and sun."

THE UNIVERSITIES' MISSION TO CENTRAL AFRICA.

VI.

THE UNIVERSITIES' MISSION TO CENTRAL AFRICA.

STIRRED by the missionary trumpet-calls of the great Livingstone in 1857, numbers of heroic souls went forth from the English Universities to give the Gospel to the African race. The time is now historic when Dr. Livingstone was accompanied by Charles Frederick Mackenzie, Archdeacon of Natal, afterwards consecrated first bishop of the mission at Cape town, January 1, 1861. In the train of these master-pioneers came a saintly band of graduates whose ordinations at Cambridge, Oxford, and Canterbury were memorable events, where the famous Bishop Wilberforce pronounced glowing benedictions on the work and the Master's servants of peace and joy.

Through the intervening years of splendid self-denial, thirty-six young men and maidens, the flower of English birth, culture, and piety,

have found rest in African graves. This martyr circle is increased by the decease of Archdeacon Goodyear, whose spirit fled at Magila,
on the 24th of June, 1889. Mournful recol-
lections entwine themselves with the vanished
years. Seldom do the voyagers up the Zambesi waterway fail to pause at the simple tomb
of Dr. Livingstone's wife, beneath the baobab
tree at Shapunga, or before the grave of Bishop
Mackenzie, at Mlolo, where the Ruo joins the
Shiré. After one brief year of sowing, the intrepid bishop fell from exposure and fatigue,
in January, 1862; his loss being greatly lamented. The inscription on the brass plate
affixed to the cross which stands over his dust
reads:

HERE LIETH

CHAS. FRED. MACKENZIE,

MISSIONARY BISHOP,

who died January 31, 1862.

"A follower of him, who was anointed to preach
deliverance to the captive, and to set at
liberty them that are bruised."

The growth of the Universities' Mission, which is closely identified with the Oxford, Cambridge, Durham, and London Universities, and the English dioceses, has been on the whole remarkably progressive. All along the line of its operations a great advance was reported during the last decade. The teaching staff, English and African, was under forty in 1880, with an annual income of £6,000; four years later, the receipts amounted to £8,000, the workers then numbering eighty. In 1888 there was a notable increase, comprising in numbers an aggregate of 1 bishop, 25 English and 2 African clergy, 25 laymen, 20 ladies, and 32 native readers and teachers—105 in all, with a financial return of £16,280. The whole of the funds are sent to the bishop, who disburses them according to his own judgment. From 1881 to 1888 a sum of £107,000 was expended in miscellaneous outlays.

For its aggressive labours there are four bases, respectively situated on the eastern shore of Lake Nyasa, with Lukoma Island as the headquarters; the Rovuma River, of which

Newala is the central station; Zanzibar Island and the Usambara country represented by Magila. Through its fourteen stations it is estimated that the influence of the mission covers an area of twenty-five thousand square miles. Principles not inferior to those of a Gregory or a Francis control its polity. These are: (1) to have no resort to civil government; (2) not to seek after political power; (3) to have nothing to do with annexation. With these are united the system of voluntary workers and of community life in its active aspect. In a debate, in 1889, in the House of Lords, on British Missionaries in East Africa, Viscount Halifax said: "There was no nobler record of work done for God, or with a more absolute and entire sacrifice of self, than was to be found in the history of that mission." To the credit of its heralds, the Universities' Mission "had already succeeded in setting a great part of the African continent moving onward in a new path."

Pioneered by Dr. Livingstone the first settlement was northeast of Blantyre, at Magomero, in July, 1861. In 1862 it was resolved, when disease had carried off Bishop Mackenzie and several comrades, to transplant the station to Chibisas on the Shiré. This spot was scarcely less disastrous and fatal. Under the direction of Bishop Tozer, the successor of Mackenzie, a sphere was chosen on Mount Morambala, adjoining the confluence of the Shiré and Zambesi. Again climatic troubles thickly befell the witness-bearers, which led Bishop Tozer to make an exodus to Zanzibar, in the hope of founding Christian homesteads on the mainland and in training redeemed slave children. It was in 1864 that the bishop was reinforced by that grand missionary, Dr. Steere, and, together, in comparative obscurity, these yokefellows from 1864 to 1874 laid broad and deep the corner-stones of the mission in the power of faith.

In 1874 Bishop Tozer resigned, exhausted and shattered in health, and the same year Edward Steere was appointed third bishop of the mission. By his polished, intellectual gifts, disciplined religious character, physical strength, and deep, human sympathies, Bishop Steere was finely endowed for the commission on which his mark has been ineffaceably stamped. With unconsumable ardour he threw himself " against the desolating ignorance and barbarism of the East African coast and the districts which supply the bulk of the slave trade." He swerved from no kind of labour. The bishop was quite as expert as carpenter, compositor, printer, bricklayer, and architect, as he was ably equipped in the departments of organising, negotiation, philology, and scholarship. Gifted with a striking personality and rare charm of address, he drew about himself a group of men having the soul of heroism, whose exalted lives and deeds were in reputation throughout East Central Africa. Early in his missionary career the bishop reduced the Swahili and Yao tongues to a written form. Dictionaries, grammars, manuals, and story-books issued from his hand, the latter entertaining the natives and familiarizing their intercourse with the Europeans. The greater labours of this apostolic man were directed to the translation into the Swahili of the New Testament, the Old Testament from Genesis to Isaiah, and the Book of Common Prayer. By Archdeacon Hodgson, who has latterly been obliged to withdraw from the mission, the unfinished translation of the Old Testament has been completed, an achievement which will lastingly associate his name with that of the distinguished bishop. Said Bishop Steere, " Our work must be all unsound without a vernacular Bible." His prolonged travels on foot in the formation of missions, visiting chiefs, rescuing slaves, and sustaining stations, well-nigh defy credibility, and, to his memory, the Slave Market Church at Zanzibar is a worthy monument. Referring to this edifice, on whose site thousands of slaves were annually sold, the late Sir Bartle Frere remarked : " It seemed to him and others as the fulfilment of a beautiful dream, which seemed hardly possible ten or twelve years ago, when he saw the market-place at Zanzibar, a filthy place, crowded with slaves, laid out side by side in hopeless despondency, without a smile on their face, without a symptom of humanity about them besides the out-

ward form. It was almost impossible to believe that where these scores and scores of
slaves were then stretched out there was now
a cathedral." In this sanctuary which the
bishop's own skill raised he (the bishop) was
buried in 1882, two years after the celebration
of the first holy communion within its walls.
It was on the 27th day of August of the same
year that Bishop Steere, a prince among missionaries, fell asleep at Zanzibar. For nine-
teen years he had served the mission, eight of
which were embraced by the bishopric. One
of those who plough deep furrows in the field
of the world's soil, his affection for East Africa
was not exceeded by the fabled love of Ulysses
for his rugged Ithaca.

Work for God was commenced in succession
at Magila, thirty miles north-west of Pangani,
and at Masasi, north of the Rovuma, and, upon
the desolation of the Masasi station in 1882 by
the terrible Magwangwara,—the vandals of the
southern Rovuma,—the headquarters of the
mission were located at Newala, 100 miles inland from the coast town of Lindi.

Eminently treading in the footsteps of Bishop Steere on the eastern shores of Nyasa, the record of the Rev. P. W. Johnson, who entered the Universities' mission field in 1876, illustrates the type of man by whom :—

" The doorways of the dark are broken."

For two years he toiled solitarily at Mwembe, until Mtaka expelled him in 1881. The year following, together with the Rev. C. A. Janson, he journeyed to Chitejis, on Lake Nyasa, where his co-labourer died. Upwards of eighteen months sadly alone and in hourly peril he proclaimed "the unsearchable riches of Christ." To his necessities the members of the Free Church at Bandawé, on the opposite coast, often ministered previous to Mr. Johnson's collapse, worn out by toilsome exertions. At Quillimane on furlough, his sight totally failed him and, on its partial restoration he embarked for England, where, by generous donations a sum of £4,000 was subscribed for the *Charles Janson* missionary vessel. A companion boat, the *Nyassa* steam-launch, has since been floated

on the blue waters of leafy-fringed Nyasa. Of
his calling this much-tried missionary has said:
" We have on the water a grand sphere of independent influence, helping chiefs and their
people; slavers and the oppressed all need help
alike, none can be lopped off by us, while none
welcome us wholly."

At Magila, the centre of the territory where
the Arabs and Germans have been oft antago-
nists, and also the region in which the Bondei
and Masai wage bloody feuds, Christianity has
won eventful triumphs. Near to these districts
are the four stations Umba, Mkuzi, Msaraka,
and Misozwe. Here invaluable help was rendered by Archdeacon Farler, whose enforced
retirement through physical weakness has been
sincerely deplored. Of this mission ground
the Earl of Dundonald wrote : " The missions
at Magila are doing a noble work. Surrounding them is a population over whom they exercise a great influence. In their churches the
heathen are taught the existence of a God;
in their schools are taught the sons of the
chiefs, who will rule over important tribes ; in

their workshops are taught useful handicrafts ; in their hospitals the sickness of the people is alleviated." Right nobly did the missionaries stand by the native Christians amid the hostilities of 1889 in their neighbourhood.

Kiungani College, for the education of a native ministry—a cherished project of Bishop Steere's—was opened in 1888. Under the shadows of the lovely St. John's Church at Mbweni, south of Kiungani, the numerous agencies employed in training and supporting hundreds of freed slaves enjoy growing prosperity. At the several mission centres the European missionaries are thus distributed : at Zanzibar, 10 ; Kiungani, 7 ; Mbweni, 10 ; Lake Nyasa, 9 ; Rovuma, 6 ; and at Magila, 18. On his visit to England in 1891, Archdeacon Maples, an admirable missionary-witness, stated that they were training a native ministry which in time would enable the English missionaries to withdraw and leave the work in the hands of African teachers and preachers. Notwithstanding their slow progress, there was a large band of African workers, both men and women, formerly released slaves, who were doing excellent service, while a native ordained minister was at present working with much greater success than any of the white missionaries.

Charles Alan Smythies, the fourth bishop, consecrated on November 30, 1883, has worn with distinction the mantle of his illustrious predecessor. His fortitude, winsomeness, self-abnegation, independence, and strength of purpose have endeared his name among fellow-messengers, kindred societies, African tribes and, not a few of the better class Arab merchants. The herculean energy of the bishop has had signal proof. On his return to England in 1888, after four years' absence, it was reported that he had made foot journeys of more than five thousand miles! His spirit of devotedness was further confirmed by his prompt re-embarkation, from furlough, for his unrepresented diocese, when apprised of the conflicts on the East Coast, where his attitude carried golden opinions. It was distressing to be informed at the close of 1891, that his health had been much enfeebled, intensified by an attack of malarial fever, causing him to write in pathetic terms, "all the strength seems to have gone out of me." Knowing that the Bishop held a living at Cardiff, Wales, in his early years, and was marked out for speedy preferment, it speaks volumes for his sacrifice and courage that he should have chosen one of the most perilous fields of service in the Dark Continent.

Every sympathy will be felt for the Mission which had to report at the beginning of 1892, a lack of volunteers, a circumstance imperilling the maintenance of important stations. This barrenness it will be hoped may only be of temporary duration. What the Mission has accomplished may be inferred from a testimony by Mr. H. H. Johnston, British Commissioner in Central Africa. He says : " In his journeyings in East Africa he had always felt, without any information or even rumours from the natives, when he was approaching the vicinity of one of the stations of the Universities' Mission. Round them there was the radiance of 'sweetness and light' and evidences of civilisation abounded."

Honour be to those who are reclaiming Afric's lost children and, by the might of the Gospel endeavouring to place their feet on the highway of salvation !

PIONEERING IN THE BAROTSI KINGDOM, ON THE UPPER ZAMBESI.

VII.

PIONEERING IN THE BAROTSI KING-
DOM, ON THE UPPER ZAMBESI.

IT was in 1877 that M. Coillard tried to
establish a missionary sphere for the Native
Churches of Basutoland among the Banyai
tribes to the north of the Limpopo River.
The fierce King of the Matabele resisted the
missionary's invasion, closed the door against
him, and, finally, to mark his intense opposition, confined M. Coillard and his friends for
a time to imprisonment. Thus baffled, the
servant of God resolved by Divine aid to make
a survey of the Barotsi Valley in the regions
and watershed skirting the Upper Zambesi.
The path of the brave-hearted man was remarkably opened to carry the Gospel to a race
speaking the Basuto tongue, a language which
they had accepted from Sebetoane and his
conquering warriors. What M. Coillard has to
record of founding a mission in the centre of

tribes "dark; chained by superstition and vice, suffering and dying," forms a chapter of service which may vie with any other in the annals of modern missions. A glimpse at the wild condition of the natives illustrates the compassionate spirit of the missionary who felt himself drawn to such people that he might have some share in hastening their deliverance from pagan barbarism. This gallant pioneer to the Barotsi pourtrays them as "treacherous and suspicious; no savages' feet are swifter than theirs to shed blood. The least provocation, the most groundless suspicion, envy, jealousy, and vengeance, justify the most atrocious crimes. Slavery has dried up the natural affections; infanticide is of too common an occurrence to shock any one; marriage is as easily dissolved as it is contracted; and the family can hardly be said to exist. Let us throw a veil over the unfathomable abyss of corruption and degradation, of which we have found a parallel nowhere in heathen Africa. The whole land is a Sodom; and these benighted people, whose conscience is dead, lit-

erally glory in their shame." A lurid picture
of heathendom which may truly call forth his
pathetic appeal, "We need to be powerfully supported, lest we grow weary under a burden too
heavy for us to bear alone." It is from this
wide field of gloomy Central Africa where no
other labourers toil that the cry "come over
and help us," derives its piercing and mournful
tones.

The Barotsi kingdom in succession to that of
the Makololo stretches from the Kafu River to
20° long. E. ; and again from the course of the
Quando and Zambesi to the watersheds of the
Congo and Zambesi. Over this scarcely known
immense tract of country upwards of 800
miles in length a comparatively sparse population is scattered, the remnants of various tribes
reduced to miserable servitude by the strong
Barotsi. Northwards, in the dense interior,
dwell countless, unvisited hordes of people
utterly ignorant of the light of God. Wars,
bloody and incessant, among the Barotsi themselves — the aristocracy of the land — have
greatly diminished the number of this race.

Many of the natives inhabit the province of Sesheke, a vast region, flat and sandy, covered with bush, and indented by several pleasant and fertile vales. Another division live in the Barotsi Valley proper, a stretch of territory consisting of an enormous lake-bed through which the Zambesi rolls. On its banks and slopes of low sand hills brushwood plentifully thrives. The riverine valley is, on an average, flooded three months annually and, at this season, the water-girt hamlets and villages standing on the islets and in the marshes are deserted by the inhabitants who pitch their camps on the upland, sand-formed hillocks. With the ebb of the flood they return to their favourite haunts on the barren plains and marshy abodes where most of their hours are spent in slothfulness and gross dissipation. The native mud hovels are filthily unclean, wretched quarters. Before these lie deep cut trenches making access to the houses almost impossible. To an imperfect extent only do the trenches drain the swampy, pestilential soil. Far as the eye can reach lagoons and marshes are seen in the driest periods of the year overgrown with rank vegetation and, consequently, under a temperature of heat at 112° or more, these spots are fever-producing hotbeds which shatter the native physique and often strike fatally the passing trader or traveller.

In 1880 and 1881 M. Coillard and Mrs. Coillard visited Europe to supply information of their former mission labours in Basutoland —famous as the scene of the life-work of that God-fearing missionary and apostle, the late Mons. Eugène Casalis—and their prospects in occupying the Barotsi Valley. From numbers of Christian friends they had the most cordial reception. In the course of this missionary campaign among the churches at home they received the heartiest co-operation from Major Malan, a true and staunch friend of the African race. Returning to the Dark Continent in May, 1882, M. and Mrs. Coillard were prevented by one obstacle after another from leaving the kingdom of the Basutos earlier than the 2d of January, 1884. Their desert journey extending over 1,000 miles, which came on the heels of a terrible drought followed by a spell of extraordinary rains, was crowded with trials and calamities. The worst of these was the loss of most of their draught bullocks through a virulent disease. On the 25th of July the missionary travellers encamped some nine miles from the flowing Zambesi, the habitat of the tsetse fly, preventing a nearer approach to the bank of the great river. M. Coillard's success in making arrangements to have an interview with King Robosi and his chiefs at the capital was shortly afterwards marred by the overthrow and flight of the king whose country became the theatre of anarchy and bloodshed. For months M. Coillard waited in suspense the tide of affairs and, on the election of a new king the missionary had the privilege of visiting his capital, Lialui, in January, 1885. The king courteously granted his guest leave to make a survey or found a station. By the 21st of August the same year the party crossed the Zambesi with their wagon and oxen and had as kindly a greeting from various chiefs who allowed them every facility of settlement over an extensive area. To reach Sesheke, 70 miles from Lishoma, these heroes literally fought their way, the thinned and famished teams of animals requiring every member of the company to put a shoulder to the wheels of the heavily-stocked wagon. Lest they should suffer from the coming rainy season or insurrectionary raids inland, Sesheke was made a present base of operations because of its situation. Apart from this it had no charms. At the time Sesheke was untenanted by any tribe. M. Coillard then spoke of it :—" The chiefs divided, fearing each other, had fled, some to the islands and others to the woods. We were left alone to battle with crocodiles, and hyenas, and other wild animals, that waged war against us night and day."

Through the succeeding years from 1885 to 1892 fresh stations have been built and numerous distant expeditions effected for the ingathering of long-neglected souls. In these endeavours M. Coillard has taken the noblest share. His deeds bear the sign-manual of rare foresight, laborious industry, and daring purpose.

He belongs to that select band of which Schiller sings :—

> " By angel trumps in heaven their praise is blown,
> Divine their lot ";

and to him a place is assigned with the mighty spirits by whom deserts are made to rejoice and blossom as the rose and kingdoms lost are again restored.

At Mambora, by the Kazangula ford, the one official entrance to the Barotsi country, were planted two Basuto evangelists and their families. M. Jeanmairit, the solitary, ordained colleague of M. Coillard,—and a missionary force, remained at Sesheke, a geographical vantage ground, and, for awhile, M. Coillard helped to promote the initial stages of the mission there previous to his departure for Sefula, 350 miles beyond. The absence of a settled population at Sesheke has made systematic Christian training and the work generally, quite impracticable. Though Sesheke happens periodically, to be the 'state' residence of fifteen chiefs,—lords of the neighbouring tribes, these swarthy rulers prefer to live independently in

their own scattered villages, leaving the capital
of their district deserted, save the care of it
to a few poor slaves. A day school was commenced which M. Jeanmairit had unwillingly
to discontinue from lack of assistance and the
absence of authority in the village. Congregations on the Lord's Day have been similarly
disappointing, their numbers being affected by
the shifting character of the native population.
Want of success in these departments has not
hindered the zealous toiler's visits to the outlying districts in order to tell of the day of
salvation. One cheering result is chronicled.
Two or three of the young chiefs have learned
to read and shew a desire to enter into the
kingdom of marvellous light. In 1887 the
Rev. L. and Mad. Jalla of the Waldensian
Church reached Sesheke and indefatigably laboured there, prior to their settlement at Kazangula, the gate of the land. To the same
destination came the young Swiss missionary,
Mons. Goy, for the purpose of affording M.
Jeanmairit a brief furlough. M. Goy will
eventually be stationed at Seoma, the Gonye

Falls, a link of importance which connects Sesheke and the Barotsi Valley. On the threshold of the country at Kazangula, Dr. Dardier fell a victim to sunstroke, "his heart and his face turned homeward." A fresh ensign, the Rev. Ad. Jalla, younger brother of Mons. L. Jalla, reached Africa in 1889 with the view of settling at a new station in the Barotsi Valley adjoining the capital. Thoroughly equipped by European training and schooled in Zambesi mission operations high anticipations are cherished of the missionary's energy and enterprise. In the autumn of 1891 the mission was reinforced by Mons. Vollet, the son of a Paris minister, accompanied by two ("we fain hope more," wrote M. Coillard) evangelists. With this rearguard the staff consists of seven missionaries, their families, and three native workers who are in occupation of three stations, to which three others as well as a couple of out-stations will shortly be added. Steadily the mission proceeds on its course, its pathways are multiplying, its leaven is spreading, and its presence creating a nobler sense of humanity.

Sefula, the headquarters of the Barotsi Mission, stands 16 miles from the capital, Lialui. On King Robosi regaining the helm of sovereignty he shewed renewed sympathy with missionary objects, and cordially invited M. Coillard to visit his royal kraal. The site of the mission centre is situated on a sand hill by which flows the modest Sefula River and is admirably adapted for educational advantages and agricultural developments. A large population dwells in the neighbourhood. At Sefula miracles of progress and civilisation are visible. A well-built church—the first seen on the Zambesi River, and a cluster of miscellaneous erections have been reared. Specially noticeable are the huts of circular arrangement, in which boys and girls receive instruction and are taught useful callings. By the practical genius of Mr. Waddell, the artisan and builder, the Sefu'a Mission structures have the look of some model European village. Mr. Waddell's dreaded antagonist is the white ant, the scourge of the African tropics, which, unchecked, speedily ruins substantial premises. For two feats

M. Coillard deserves congratulation—a useful canal and an excellent roadway. In conjunction with Nguana Ngombe, the earliest Barotsi convert, a young man of talent and fine resolution,—M. Coillard had pleasure, after two years of toil, in seeing at the close of 1891, the canal triumphantly completed. Admittedly a missionary waterway, it is 10 miles in length, joining the Sefula station and the broad Zambesi's course. Transports, goods, passengers, etc., are carried on the surface of the canal and the entire valley is now directly influenced by Christianising civilisation. The upper sources of the river cleared, a stronger volume of water will be available. Towards this appreciated neck of communication an English gentleman liberally contributed most of the required funds. The missionaries, Mr. and Mrs. Jalla, were the first to sail Zambesi-wards on the miniature Suez from visiting M. Coillard, who said concerning the event :—" It may well be imagined with what feelings we accompanied our beloved friends to the landing at the foot of the hill, and with what interest our eyes followed

their boats gliding gently down the stream."
This achievement has not wholly removed the
isolation of the missionary sentinel. A post
seldom arrives more than once a year and the
problem of conveying supplies from Mangwato
to Kazangula, the nearest point of the Zambesi, and thence to Sefula, remains practically
unsolved, notwithstanding the road, or rather
wagon *track*, which M. Coillard laid from Sesheke to Sefula, over 350 miles long across
sandy plains and through thick forests. Infested with the tsetse fly and the recurring
growth of poisonous plants, so ruinous to cattle,
this track has been forsaken and the river fallen
back upon for transit. Smooth sailing here is
not possible owing to the numerous rapids
and the Gonye Falls. To conquer these obstacles and to be relieved of the necessity of using
the small, leaky canoes which are as expensive
as dangerous, M. Coillard purposes securing
two moderately sized launches of a ton each,
one of these to ply above and the other below
the Gonye Falls.

Unfaltering in spirit M. Coillard has served

seven years in the Zambesian Regions. He describes the land as " fallow ground which, for a long time yet, we shall have to break up." Tribal warfare in many of the deadly climates is attended by shocking barbarities, and in its train polygamy of the most debasing kind, slavery with its horrible cruelties, superstition which burns alive its helpless victims, and all the abominations of lying, theft, and murder. To deliver the youth of these degraded beings M. Coillard who has given himself specially to evangelising opened a school. The few books and slates and a slender staff necessarily limited the progress. More regretably the pupils, mostly young chiefs with their slave attendants, revolted against the least discipline. " The village which they built," says M. Coillard, " and over which we can have no control, was a den of thieves and the hotbed of the grossest shameless immorality. They feared no one and respected nothing. They impudently rode our donkeys to death in broad daylight: stole cloth, food, tools, everything they could get hold of—even things which were utterly useless to them, such as barometers and thermometers; and what in the house was beyond their reach they found no difficulty in inducing our servants to steal for them." M. Coillard earnestly pursued his mission nobly aided by a devoted partner and, in three years' time several of the young men learned to read and enjoyed the perusal of a New Testament and hymn book. On the arrival of a box of these not a few of the royal pupils each brought a calf in exchange for a copy of the Testament while the destitute slaves cheerfully toiled in order to possess the same treasure. Afterwards the school was popular, its order preserved, and its atmosphere changed. Litia, the eldest son of the reigning King Lewanika, has been sent with five other promising scholars to the Morija High School, Basutoland. Ten girls have entered the Sefula schools, five of whom are kings' daughters and nieces, whose clothing and food beside tuition make a heavy demand on the mission's limited resources. It is disappointing to M. Coillard that he has often to decline the applications of dark little fellows because there is no instructor. Late in 1891 a deep shadow fell upon this hopeful branch of service. To the constant strain of teaching the pupils who had increased from 30 to 40 to about 100, Madame Coillard, a woman of rare spiritual beauty, succumbed. Shattered in health Madame Coillard stood to the end at the post of sacred duty. Fittingly may the Church of God say to her:—

> "Sleep sweetly, tender heart, in peace;
> Sleep, holy spirit, blessed soul,—
> Sleep till the end, true soul and sweet,
> Sleep full of rest from head to feet."

Most providentially the school work has been taken up by Miss Kiener, a Swiss lady, who reached the confines of Zambesi-land ere the supplicating M. Coillard was aware of her coming.

A brighter outlook appears on the horizon of Zambesia, and much countenance is given to it by the king's improved attitude, customs, and decrees. He forbids the sale of liquor in his capital and is himself an abstainer; he has stopped that awful form of administering poison to unfortunate creatures accused of witchcraft and then burning their bodies; he has prohibited his people selling slaves to the Portuguese from the west coast; and, for four years he has not offered a human sacrifice or allowed his subjects to practise this rite. The peaceable aims of the missionaries are understood and, although their property has been ruthlessly pillaged no hand has ever attempted to take their lives. To the pleas of the heralds of the kingdom savage natures even pay greater regard and at the services on the Lord's Day worshippers more regularly congregate. The mission station is a centre of illumination. A new missionary expedition of the English Primitive Methodists recently to Mashikulomboe Land led by Mr. Buckenham and its occupation of a location in the king's territory is a stimulus to holy aggression.

Under the direction of the Paris Evangelical Missionary Society and French in tongue the Zambesi Mission is international otherwise. From the ordinary funds of the Society no aid is obtained. It is dependent upon the people of God in many lands including the nationalities of France, Holland, Switzerland, England,

Scotland, and Basutoland and, to its worthy claims friends have generously responded to smooth the path and lighten the burden of its leader whose entreaty is, "forget not this part of Africa." The fruitfulness of its career brings proportionate obligation and incites to a loftier faith on behalf of the heathen world. Of what spirit Mons. Francois Coillard is made one glimpse is offered. Writing in 1891 he says:—"I have lost my only horse—the gift of a friend—and a horse here is a fortune, an acqui-sition beyond our means. But, though no longer young, I am ready cheerfully to tramp the burning sand and the deep mud, under this torrid sun, to make known, as far as I can, the glad tidings of salvation." By this type of Christian manhood embracing patriotism in its widest sense the Apostle Paul's injunction is eloquently fulfilled, " Remember them that are in bonds, as bound with them," and the hap-pier time brought nigh of which a poet has sung :—

"In that sweet day when none shall ask another
'What blood is thine, in what ancestral skin?'"

SUNRISE IN KAFRARIA, SOUTH AFRICA.

VIII.

SUNRISE IN KAFRARIA, SOUTH AFRICA.

AMONG the half dozen principal territories likely to be included in the future South African Republic, Kafraria, which lies on the immediate south-eastern coast of Africa, is already an acknowledged valuable possession of Great Britain. Previous to 1820 the country was practically unvisited and, for years afterwards, a few scattered traders and pioneer missionaries were the solitary inhabitants. Following its complete British occupation, the history of Kafraria assumed a new complexion and, latterly, colonisation and missionary extensions have travelled steadily abreast. In former days when the Kafirs and English were in conflict the mission stations were often attacked and destroyed. Energetically the missionaries rebuilt the stations and, under a civilised rule, they now enjoy a permanent existence. A new chapter is opening, and, from the Cape to Natal,—northeast of Kafraria, and, as far northwards as the Limpopo River, the mission settlements of the European and American societies dot the soil ; a noble proof that Christianity is heroically banishing the face of heathen darkness.

Civilisation is springing in the footsteps of the messengers of the Cross. The day of roads, a sign of intercourse and progress, has arrived. Far and wide the miserable, rugged tracks of a generation ago are covered by broad highways, while the railway system, another agent of civilising power, has daily expansion. Cape Colony is intersected with hundreds of miles of the iron road, the chief line stretching from Cape Town to Kimberley. The old-time journeys of Moffat, weeks in duration, to Bechuanaland, with wagon and in-spanned oxen, are at present made in three or four days.

In the article of clothing another index of advance, the Christian Kafir generally dons himself in semi-English garb or, if less progressive wears a superior blanket about his smeared body. For domestic convenience he readily uses pots, pails, and plates of foreign manufacture and, instead of the archaic, primitive, wooden spade, with which he was accustomed to scratch, or, as has been said, "tickle," the earth, he prefers the iron hoe. Dexterously he follows the light American plough, a species of import, the surplus home-profits on which, would pay twice over the cost of the existing staff of missionaries. Most people have heard something of the quaint, rude, Kafir hut. In every part of the country these single-roomed, grass-covered, bee-hive shaped creations with one division were once visible rising from the earth. Their day is sinking into oblivion. The successors of these, plainly suggestive of Western architecture, rest on strong supports, with plastered walls, and, most valuable of all, having a couple or more of sections. Whether grouped in isolated lots in South Kafraria or, in the big towns of the interior, the kraals of the Kafirs are yielding to the impress of the white man's hand and designs.

Woman's elevation, a distinct stamp or product of Christian influence, is witnessed. Yesterday, the wife of a heathen Kafir was the usual, solitary figure at work in the hut or down the brown burnt furrows and, to her was entrusted the unpleasant task of settling her husband's disputes with the head-man of the tribe. Meanwhile her "master," lazily lounged by the cattle, smoked his pipe, and took charge of the young children from morning till sunset. Alluding to women's work, a missionary at the Amaxesibe Mission says:—"Women and children are expected to do all the work,—they are the hewers of wood and drawers of water; the children,—the herds and weeders, the milkers, the grinders, the nurses,—in fact, everything they can do, and many things they cannot. It is a common sight to see a little lad trying to guide a plough drawn by six fractious oxen, while the father or elder brother quietly looks on, with scarcely a hand to help. It takes the women a whole day to go to the bush, six or eight miles off, chop a bundle of wood, and carry it back on the head. These bundles vary in size according to the strength of the bearer;

but some, weighed at the store out of curiosity, turned the balance at over 80 lbs." The practice of the converted Kafir, who labours on his "location," ploughs and sows, weeds and reaps, is otherwise. He scorns to make his partner a rough toiler in the fields, preferring to do it himself or, with male assistance. The diet of the Kafir both in range and quality has not been unaffected. For a generation, acres of golden corn have been raised and much of it exported over the seas, its cultivation marking a superior stage to milk, flesh, and mealies, the earlier and sole means of subsistence. Compared with his paltry trading half a century ago the Kafir's present exports amount to several thousands of pounds annually. The Kafir's fierce enemies of the plains and bushy ravines,—lions, tigers, hyenas, and kindred quadruped, have nearly bade him good-bye, and each year the agricultural prospect of the Kafir is brightening and improving. This cheery picture is not free from shadows. The evils of centuries of unrelieved heathenism work terrible havoc. In hearts unconquered by Christ, lying, thieving, adultery, witchcraft, and polygamy, aboundingly prevail, the two latter being formidable adversaries. The beer drinking of the Kafirs is notorious. In the vicinity of towns the Kafir drinks freely of the white man's beer, which is more ruinous than his native-made beverage. Both men and women smoke constantly and where the Kafir can escape the demands of work he is quite as willing as the rest of humanity to avail himself of the ease of indolence.

On all hands education is regarded a blessing of immense advantage, the foundation of coming prosperity, and a prime auxiliary of the gospel of the kingdom. Where in the last generation it was almost impossible for the missionary to persuade the parents to send their children to school it has become the custom of the young people to seek admission into the Government and Mission schools. Every year the British Government is erecting additional schools for the native race and the spectacle of thousands of the young attending the excellent Scottish missionary institutions at

Lovedale, Blythswood, Healdtown, Grahams-town, and elsewhere, is an augury of a nation-hood of sons and daughters whose lives will be fashioned upon the Master's divine pattern. Much interest attached to the departure of Sekhomi the only son of Khama in 1892, for training at Lovedale College. Khama, a con-vert of the London Missionary Society, the chief paramount of Bechuanaland, and, unques-tionably, the most intelligeut, enlightened, and progressive of South African chiefs, was de-sirous that his son should have an English education. For this purpose he requested Sir Henry Loch, the High Commissioner, to place Sekhomi in a school of first rank. Sekhomi was met at Vryburg and conducted to Love-dale, by Mr. Theal, the historian of South Africa, and one of the foremost officials in the Native Affairs Office. A number of promising Bechuana youths are enjoying the benefits of Lovedale. By the choice of this college for Khama's son's education, the High Commis-sioner paid a highly deserved tribute to that worthy South African educational reformer, Dr.

Stewart,—a modern Comenius, whose name,
future generations of South African natives
and settlers will hold in grateful remembrance.
It is intended that Lovedale shall be the model
of the Industrial College which the British East
Africa Company have decided to establish in
their territory on the Kibwezi River, at an
altitude of three thousand feet, in the neighbourhood of good water, fertile soil, plenty of
timber, and in the centre of a populous and
friendly district. Dr. Stewart, who went in
search of a site for this New Lovedale at the
request of Sir William Mackinnon and Mr. A.
L. Bruce (Dr. Livingstone's son-in-law), states
that the heathen natives at Kibwezi have never
before seen the face of a white man except
that of a stray traveller or Arab invader and
cannot divine what intention the Scotchman
has of seeking a settlement in their midst.

For the tuition of Kafir youths as much as
£8 per annum is frequently expended in order
that they may have instruction in elementary,
advanced, and technical branches; many of
them afterwards become skilled artisans, teach-

ers, and lawyers, and some as missionaries bear the Cross to the dark tribes of Central Africa. In the schools English is taught and, in the same tongue the natives talk to the settlers. Native letters too, pass in thousands through the Cape post, an indication of the times, while a goal of Kafir ambition is to rent ground or to have a wagon for the conveyance of his own or a trader's goods. Among valued imports,—the Angora goat, the horse, milk-giving cattle, and wool-bearing sheep, undreamt of fifty years back, are the principal stock.

Far and away, the missionary, uniting in himself the functions of educator, philanthropist, organiser, and preacher, is the best of the Kafir's friends. To him the Kafir is evermore a debtor. Though the missionary may not receive hearty expressions of native gratefulness he has his reward in more gratifying forms. He sees old settlements becoming self-supporting, ardent Kafir evangelists, schools and churches, over the landscape, which severally indicate that pioneering days in Kafirland may be past, in the span of another generation.

Honour is eminently due to the Free Church
and United Presbyterian Scotch missionary
societies for their services on behalf of the
social, educational, and religious training of the
Kafir race. Were the episodes in the history
of their great work written in detail some vivid
chapters would be given to the Christian
Church. Missionaries of the stamp of Stirling,
Lundie, and Shearer, have splendidly honoured
their calling :—

"to sow the seed, and reap the harvest with enduring
toil."

It has been said of that gifted missionary-
teacher, the Rev. J. D. Don, M.A., of King
William's Town, representing the Free Church,
that, " his commanding influence has ever been
thrown on the side of the Kafir and the mission in the colonist controversies on native
questions. By his public vindication of Kafir
life and rights in 1885, he did 'a deed which
places him in the notable ranks of Christian
missionaries and philanthropists who have suffered bonds and even death in the cause of
justice to the slave and the oppressed.'"

These, and like fellow workers and, of " honour-able women not a few," have exhibited indus-try, foresight, and masterly perseverance, not unworthy of the highest tributes of praise.

The Kafir's musical ear, faculty, and voice, have deserved reputation. With drilling they excel as singers and in the part-singing of hymns they combine sweetness and harmony. In their own land they often charm the Euro-pean settlers by their quaint, melodious, and expressive songs. Of their vocal gifts evidence was afforded in 1891–2 by the visit of the South African Choir to Great Britain for the purpose of illustrating the training received at the mission institutions and also the procuring of funds for the establishment of technical schools in South Africa in which handicrafts may be taught the young men and domestic economy, nursing, cooking, etc., to young women. These interesting visitors of varied shades of colour and dressed in native costume represented seven distinct branches of the Kafir race belonging to the Amaxosa, Fingo, Tembu, Bapedi, Basuto, Zulu, and Cape tribes.

The writer had the pleasure of entertaining three of the ladies whose brightness, polite demeanour, intelligence, and Christian earnestness, did great credit to the labour of the missionaries.

No definite forecast of this race, the most remarkable in the South African Continent, can be given. In South Africa the best judgment widely prevails that where the Kafirs adopt the false civilisation of Europe they are doomed to extermination and, on the other hand, that, in accepting the Christian faith, a bright career is before them. It is usual for traders and farmers to ridicule the Kafir's profession of Christianity. The assumption is made that every native in European dress is necessarily a Christian and, if he happens to cheat or steal, it is placed to the discredit of missions. Rarely however has it been found when such cases have been made the subjects of inquiry that the accused ever held a church member's certificate. With respect to the wish of farmers to have the services of raw Kafirs rather than Christians the missionaries boldly reply that it is because the farmer more easily trades on the ignorance and servility of a "Red" *i.e.* heathen Kafir, who is content with the lowest wages, whereas the self-respecting native declines these terms.

Steadily the evangelisation of the unfixed Kafir races is continued. Of the 650,000 Kafirs in Cape Colony, about one-fourth have been baptised and, in Zululand, of 50,000, upwards of 2,000 are Christians. In the independent kingdom of Pondoland, out of 150,000 at least 3,000 are Christianised natives. When spiritual returns from Kafir Missions are under examination the broad, racial characteristics of the race need to be set distinctly within view. Says the Moravian *Missionsblatt* of the Kafir, as he is seen in the Tembu tribes: " He has redeeming traits, clearly discernible traces, though sadly marred and discontinuous, of the original imprint of God's similitude. But, on the other hand, assuredly he is far from being that uncorrupted, harmless child of nature that dimly, dreaming worshippers of man would make him out to be. No; his true portrait does not merely include individual shadows and unclean disfiguring spots, but the whole foundation of his moral being is awry, untrue, impure, and unholy, plainly attesting his indispensable need of the redemption in Christ, that only through the energy of grace and the inner transformation wrought thereby can he be restored to his true temporal and eternal destiny." Towards the salvation of the Kafir the missionary at every civilisatory stage witnesses with joy that heathen customs are being forsaken or practised only in secret places. The missionary's station is a fountain for desert hearts. From it flow the streams by which the life-destinies of a great people are being triumphantly altered. What surprising changes would greet the eyes of the early labourers of seventy years ago on Kafrarian fields were they to return again! By them the seed was cast into the sterile ground and, to-day, before the reapers, rises the harvest of God waiting His servants' garnering hands.

PLANTING THE FLAG OF MISSIONS IN KATANGA.

IX.

PLANTING THE FLAG OF MISSIONS IN KATANGA.

POSSESSED of those well known Scottish qualities, hardihood and tenacity, Frederick Stanley Arnot,—pioneer, explorer, and missionary, has given fresh emphasis to the saying, that the cause of Missions will not permit any land to lie untilled. With the love of souls which

" fires fainting wills, and builds heroic minds,"

Arnot was roused by one of Livingstone's farewell speeches in Scotland, in the year 1864; from which date he consecrated himself to the claims of the heathen world. Mastered by the passion that "the most worthy pursuit is the prosperity of the whole world," the young knight-errant of the faith reached the East African coast in 1881, to begin his eminently honoured career. Forcing a passage through

the territories of savage potentates in the teeth
of enormous difficulties, Mr. Arnot ultimately
won an entrance into Msidi's kingdom as the
first missionary of the Cross and received from
the venerable African chief a very friendly au-
dience. Msidi's dominions lying to the west
of Lakes Moero and Bangweolo and south of
the Congo Free State, embrace an immense
area of country. Previous to Mr. Arnot's arrival at the capital, Europeans had found admission impossible. The dusky monarch is by
far the greatest ruler in that part of the Dark
Continent, his possessions standing on the
ruins of the ancient kingdoms of the Muata
Cazembe and the Muata Janow. In acquiring
a protectorate over Katanga and obtaining
concessions from Msidi two European nations
are putting forward claims. Katanga, it seems,
lies on the disputed western border land between the country recently declared by Lord
Salisbury to be under British influence, and
the vast African territory of the King of the
Belgians. Portugal's supposed rights in Katanga are wholly ignored.

Mr. Arnot began his adventurous march into the dark interior by journeying from Natal to Shoshong, whence he intended crossing the desert on foot joined by native boys and three donkeys. So hazardous a step was prevented by Khama, a Christian chief of reputation, generously equipping the Scotchman with wagons and a score of oxen, a body of native helpers, and, also accompanying the expedition for a long distance himself. Battling with many perils and trying reverses Mr. Arnot arrived at the Chobe River and afterwards trudged on to Panda-ma-tenka, where he was attacked by a virulent fever. Had a noble African lad not nursed him with untiring fidelity his life would undoubtedly have been forfeited. On recovering Mr. Arnot was kindly aided by the chief Lewanika, who conveyed the white man in his canoes up the broad, shining waters of the Zambesi. Naturally this chief was keenly disappointed when the recipient of his favours declined to make a permanent residence at his capital. Travelling westerly Mr. Arnot fell in with the Bakuti, amongst whom for a few days he had striking evangelising experiences. Acquainted with their dialect the missionary preached Christ to some purpose and opened the kingdom of heaven to the dark barbarians. Other native receptions were less cheering. Further to the west he and his small company were raided by a tribe who burnt the grass around their tent and carried off eight followers. In a plucky fashion Mr. Arnot went in search of his kidnapped natives, an adventure which he has brightly described. " There was nothing to do but to find their trail and follow them up. After a ten miles' journey we reached a little village in the forest where they were resting. They thought we had come to fight with them, and they rushed out with their guns, bows and arrows, and spears, to receive us. My men, thirty or forty in number, being only Africans, got in fighting order, and began to load their guns for action. I was a little way behind, and did not take in the situation at once. Seeing how things were going, I ran forward, seized a little stool and held it up in the air as a signal of peace. This arrested the

enemy, and at last two of them, seeing me
seated, came forward to hear what I had to
say. After a little talk, it turned out that the
whole thing was a mistake. They thought we
had come to their country to rob and plunder
them, and quite naturally, in self-defence, they
wished to have the first hit at us. Next day
we spent the time in receiving presents, and
telling them of the things we had been speaking to the people all along the road." Resum-
ing his journey Mr. Arnot traversed a seldom
trodden region and, at length reached Bihé.
Of the Biheans, with whom he stayed for a time,
he furnishes numerous interesting sketches.
His next stage was to Benguella, on the West
African coast. His arrival there was a sufficient proof that Grant, Cameron, and others
had a successor, who dared, with only a scanty
escort, to cross the great African Continent.

Undeterred by the narrow escapes and weary
tramping Mr. Arnot struck inland once more
after enjoying a brief rest. Resolved at all
hazards to reach Msidi's capital the young
Scotchman, with amazing energy, fought his

way pacifically into the very heart of the
Garenganze country and achieved in the interests of Christianity, what at a later date was
accomplished for purposes of commerce and
colonisation by Lieutenant Le Marinel, an en-
voy of the Congo Free State, to whom the
honour belongs of commanding the first expedition which penetrated as far as Msidi's capital. Msidi warmly countenanced the proposals
of Mr. Arnot, whose labours, similar to Mackay's in Uganda, broadly consisted of initiating
Christian civilisation. Year after year this
civilising pioneer exhibited strenuous activity
in advancing the elementary conditions of
progress, industrial pursuits, and, as devotedly,
illustrated the Gospel message. By his teaching and character Mr. Arnot was winning
favour in the eyes of the natives and, in heroic
fashion preparing the way for comrades and
successors. He was endeavouring to exemplify
the counsel which the Patriarch of African
Missions addressed to him on the point of departure for Africa. This was:—" Have patience, patience, patience, and then you will suc-

ceed." Two brother missionaries,—Mr. C. A.
Swan, of Sunderland, England, and, Mr. W. L.
Faulknor, from Canada, were welcomed to
Katanga, in 1887, and, on their settlement Mr.
Arnot, after a chequered seven years' history
in Darkest Africa, returned to Great Britain in
1888, where before large audiences in geographical and Christian circles he recounted the development of Garenganze. In England Mr.
Arnot married Miss H. J. Fisher and, together
with her and a band of strong-souled fellow-
workers, the good soldier of faith sailed in
1890 for his adopted country and, has subsequently located himself temporarily, at Bihé,
on the line of route between the coast and
Katanga.

Onward from 1887 until the time of his furlough home in 1892 Mr. Swan most ably
directed the extension of missionary work in
the kingdom of Garenganze. His love for the
children, his perception of native peculiarities,
his unflinching assertion of justice, and his
sowing of Divine truth severally contributed to
the success of Mr. Swan's enterprise. On the

journey from the West Coast of Africa' to the interior he had a full share of difficulties including four attacks of fever and, was vexingly delayed by powerful chiefs who demanded cloths, powder, guns, etc. These chiefs were terrible despots whose orders, however unjust they might be, the people dare not refuse, knowing that any resistance would be visited with death. Msidi, the King of Katanga, had thousands of wives. So numerous were these Amazons that Mr. Swan spoke of them being " about as plentiful as the rain-drops." Mainly through this body Msidi ruled his subjects. Every important village had one of these women, who, besides receiving tribute, kept the chief posted up with what occurred. For all kinds of offences, whether great or small, the penalty of capital punishment was rigorously enforced. Greatly as the inhabitants of Garenganze delighted in battle and were of a warlike temperament they were exceedingly industrious and skilled workers in copper and other materials. In religious matters the natives had strange ideas of a Supreme Being in whom they firmly believed as controlling the destinies of men. Fetichism and witchcraft had a strong hold upon them; no one was supposed to die a natural death. Revolting cruelties were inflicted and, the horrible look of the villages, the defences of which were surmounted by human skulls, did not give the traveller or missionary a comfortable feeling. For three years Mr. Swan and Mr. Faulknor were the solitary white missionaries in the country and, during that time they only received three mails from England. Three more missionaries afterwards entered Garenganze, Messrs. Laing, Thompson, and Crawford, who had a hearty greeting from the chief and the natives. When Mr. Swan purposed leaving for a home-sojourn Msidi, considering him a great friend, refused to allow the missionary's departure. Eventually Mr. Swan's exit was effected by the arrival of the staff of a Congo Free State expedition. He joined the returning caravan and, in 68 days reached the first Congo station, thence sailed down the waters of the Congo, and, in six weeks' time set foot on British shores, having been away from England exactly six years and seventeen days. The distance from the West Coast of Africa to Garenganze was 900 miles, the journey occupying upwards of four months.

Of Lieutenant Le Marinel, the young Belgian officer who was in the service of the Free State and the first traveller to reach Bunkeia, from the Congo, Mr. Swan speaks in the kindliest terms. With this officer Mr. Swan journeyed back to the Congo River. Le Marinel's expedition has been productive of valuable data respecting the geographical and ethnological characteristics of the regions traversed. He crossed the basin of three rivers—the Sankourou, Lomami, and the Lualaba, and passed through rich and fertile lands not previously trodden by white men's footsteps. Tribes of savages were seen who painted their faces in loud-toned hues and their entire bodies on special occasions; their hair being folded up into thick mats and coloured with mingled dyes. These natives were extremely ignorant of anybody or anything outside their own immediate domains and, unacquainted with the art of war. They contented themselves in the petty feuds of individuals and families. Msidi saluted Le Marinel in a cordial spirit, having the impression that his visitor would supply him with powder and ammunition for use against some of his rebellious subjects. On discovering that Le Marinel's good offices were limited to expressions of loyal friendship and did not include the sinews of war, the monarch's attitude changed for a time. Prior to Le Marinel returning to the Congo amicable relations were again established. The Belgian explorer found that the earlier reports of Msidi's declining health were confirmed. He had reigned for a long period, was in old age, very feeble, and broken in spirit. For many years he had objected to have the slightest intercourse with white men before the missionaries gained his esteem and secured permission to settle in his capital. Since the month of June, 1891, when Le Marinel left Msidi's territory nothing was heard of the patriarchal chief until the arrival of a brief telegram in April, 1892, announcing that Msidi, the King of Katanga, had been deposed, an event probably not unconnected with the advance of the four trading expeditions upon Katanga. Following his return to England Mr. Swan, the missionary, at the invitation of the King of the Belgians travelled to Brussels, to give His Majesty such information as he possessed bearing on the kingdom over which Msidi has ruled for several years.

Fruitless attempts were made from the south, in 1890–1, to enter Katanga. A daring traveller, Mr. A. Sharpe, one of Mr. H. H. Johnston's vice-consuls, and whose journeys of exploration in Central Africa have been signally successful, tried to reach Katanga to present the credentials of Great Britain. On this errand the expeditionary party suffered terrible hardships in the countries adjoining Msidi's dominions. Baffled for awhile Mr. Sharpe made interesting discoveries north of Lake Moero and, moving afterwards, in a south-westerly direction, entered Cazembe's capital. In this ferocious potentate's country where human sacrifices are of frequent occurrence Mr. Sharpe had the hospitality of a barbaric ruler for eight days.

The traveller was informed that during the last one hundred years only four Europeans had visited Cazembe's land. Mr. Sharpe was able to verify the stories of the rich gold deposits to the south of Lake Moero, which may possibly result in the state becoming the centre of a flourishing mining industry. Notwithstanding the obstacles which Cazembe planted in the way of Mr. Sharpe getting into Msidi's capital, the explorer had the satisfaction of seeing the wily, old monarch, though he does not appear in the course of the six days' interview to have had a gracious reception or received special material advantages. About the same period Mr. Joseph Thomson was endeavouring to set foot in Katanga. To Mr. Thomson's misfortune, most of his followers were struck down with small-pox, which prevented the distinguished traveller from penetrating Msidi's kingdom. Much interest is excited in the prospects of the four exploring parties approaching Garenganze in 1892. Captain Stairs, one of Stanley's former officers, was commanding a force from the east coast for exploration and imposing the suzerainty of the Congo Free State and Anglo-Belgian Katanga Company over Msidi's provinces; Lieutenant Dhanis was leading a second; the Delcommune expedition was going inland from Ngongo-Lutita; and, Captain Bia, starting in November, 1891, was in charge of a fourth, journeying by the route which Lieutenant Le Marinel opened.

Of what may be termed African Folk-Lore relating to tribes living westward of Katanga, Mr. Swan pens useful jottings which point to the origin of some of the names borne by African races. Says the missionary of natives in the neighbourhood of the river Lubi, when he was travelling with Le Marinel :—

"Not far distant from these parts many of the Luba people have the combination 'Bashila' in their family name—for instance, the Bashilange (Kalamba's people), Bashilambwa, Bashilanzefu. M. Le Marinel and I were talking over the probable meaning of the combination. We knew that Ba was a plural prefix, but it was not until after some thought that I remembered that the word shila (sometimes chila or jila) is that which the Luba people use for 'antipathy.' If I were to ask the Yeke people why they do not eat zebra flesh, they would reply, 'Chijila'—*i. e.*, 'It is a thing to which we have an antipathy,' or, perhaps,

better, 'It is one of the things which our fathers
taught us not to eat.' The Biheans use the word chi-
kola to express the same thing. The words nge,
mbwa, nzefu, in the above combinations mean respectively leopard, dog, elephant. So it seems as
though the word Bashilange means 'the people who
have an antipathy to the leopard'; the Bashilambwa,
'those who have an antipathy to the dog'; and the
Bashilanzefu, 'those who have an antipathy to the
elephant.' We called a native, and, after a great deal
of questioning, he understood what we were driving
at, and we found our conclusion to be correct. He
then told us how the Bashilambwa and the Bashilanzefu got their names. At one time they were only
known as the Bashilambwa, because they considered
it was wrong to eat the dog. But one day a number
of them went across the Lubi River to hunt elephants,
and stayed many days, during which rains had fallen,
the river became much swollen, and when the hunters
returned they could not cross. While they were won-
dering what to do an elephant came past, and, seeing
that they were troubled, asked what was the matter.
They were all much surprised, of course, to hear the
elephant speak. But it went on, saying they must
not be surprised, for it was a human being like themselves ; they could not cross the river, but it could
very easily, and advised them to get on its back, which
they did, and reached the other side in safety. Ever
since that time they have refused to eat the flesh
of the elephant, and are now known as the Bashilanzefu."

Contributions of this class which bear on the

customs, traditions, and philology of strange peoples are always welcomed. In the same section of investigation Dr. Turner, Dr. Inglis, and a number of eminent South Sea missionaries have collected facts illustrative of Polynesian races which Professor Max Müller, Sir H. Tylor, and scientific scholars have much appreciated.

By enthusiastically uplifting the missionary cross the outlook in the kingdom of Garenganze has distinct promise, for which the lives of some of the missionaries have been laid down. At the threshold of the campaign the names of martyrs are inscribed on its " bede " roll. That tragic, yet sublime declaration of an African missionary :—" Ah ! I am one of those men whose dead bodies will fill the trench to make it easier for others to come after us, and walk over us, and take the citadel," has an eloquent enforcement in the mission annals of Garenganze. Through such sacrifices the dawn is breaking on darkest regions and the prospect of a better day already appears on the horizon. Severe is the calling of men and women at Equatorial African out-posts who are "painfully plodding on in their frequently thankless task of impregnating the dull minds of Africans sodden with barbarism, with the light of religious ideas." All that men most admire has exhibition on these far away fields in the conflicts of faith. Zeal, earn-estness, trust, and self-abnegation are the hall-marks of these ambassadors of love. They have seen and responded to the observation of Mr. Stanley that, "the time has come and the hour has struck for civilisation to enter Africa, to remember the blessing of Living-stone, and in the name of God and the Chris-tian nations, to steer right onward." It must be that in God's own season these scenes of labour shall become the witnesses of growingly fragrant toil.

MISSIONARY ADVANCE UP THE CONGO WATERWAY.

.

X.

MISSIONARY ADVANCE UP THE CONGO WATERWAY.

FOURTH in magnitude of the great African rivers, the Congo, which Stanley announced to the world on his arrival at Boma in 1877 to be identical with the Lualaba of the interior, and partially explored by Livingstone, has become in little over one decade a principal missionary and trading sphere of the Dark Continent. The Lower Congo,—from its mouth, terminates at the Falls of Yellala, whence the second stage— the Middle Congo—reaches to Stanley Pool, a distance of 350 miles from the Atlantic Ocean. Above Stanley Pool opens the Upper Congo, extending to Stanley Falls, 1,500 miles inland, and, far beyond into the depths of Africa. For 940 miles this latter section is navigable. On the lower parts of the river, Puerto da Lenha, once had notoriety for the slave ships which arrived there to receive thousands of cargoes of slaves for shipment to other shores, and, some 31 miles higher up the river stands Boma, in picturesque surroundings, formerly the greatest slave market in the world. Several stations were planted in succession on the Congo by Stanley for the Comité des Etudes du Haut. The first of the five leading stations was established at Vivi, 115 miles from the sea, the portal of the new country, followed at intervals by Isanghila, Stanley Pool, Leopold-ville, Ibaka, and a number of auxiliary stations.

In 1891 it was calculated that the foreign population of the State of which Boma is the capital, numbered 800, mostly of European nationalities, and, of the 72 English and 35 Swedes, the greater part—over 80 in all—were missionaries. The opening of the Congo railroad from Matadi, to the Leopold Ravine, is a strong link of union towards the furtherance of intercourse and commercial relations between the whites and the natives. Civilisation too, will rapidly follow in its track and slavery receive a staggering blow. For the slave trade and the locomotive to exist side by side in Africa is an utter impossibility.

The year 1878, *annus mirabilis* in African missionary records, marks the entrance of the English Baptists into the Congo Valley. Of the pioneers' fourteen years of struggle only fragmentary narratives have been published, yet enough has come to light to establish their claims upon the gratitude and admiration of the Christian Church. Soldiers and heroines of faith they have served, suffered, and, often laid down their lives in the endeavour to satisfy the lifelong hunger of Congo's millions. It is not forgotten that when the Baptist Missionary Society presented the renowned explorer, Mr. Stanley, with an address seven years ago at a public breakfast in London he spoke in eloquent terms of the Baptist missionaries and their American fellow-toilers on the Congo. For their progress Mr. Stanley had rendered esteemed co-operation which added to his eulogy of the missionaries as " labourers who toiled as he had seen them much more severely than he could do in the heart of Africa, many of them being bright examples of the blessing to be derived from honest work." Of the Bap-

tist death-roll on the Congo it had been said:
"no Christian Church had supplied a nobler
contingent to the army of martyrs." In this
martyr circle the name of Comber, is mourn-
fully illustrious, embracing the missionaries—
Dr. Sidney Comber, Mr. Thomas J. Comber,
Mrs. Hay, her sister, Mrs. Thomas J. Comber,
then, Mrs. Percy Comber, who reached Africa
in May, 1890, and, some months later fell a
victim to the malarious climate. Sorrow over
this last sacrifice had not ceased ere the sad intelligence reached England in March, 1892, that
the Rev. Percy E. Comber, surviving his young
wife only by twelve months, had succumbed to
the terrible African fever ; his death chivalrously
crowning a pathetic episode in the history of
the Congo Mission. The Combers,—three
brothers, one sister, and two wives,—six in all,
a noble, self-sacrificing family, dying on the
Congo in the cause of missions, present a
martyrs' page not eclipsed even in the martyrdoms of apostolic days. Dr. Maclaren justifia-
bly said at the Liverpool gathering in celebra-
on of the Baptist Missionary Centenary Fund

that the Baptist Society had claims for support on the ground of the many martyrs and saints who had gained possession of Africa with their blood ; and of the Congo, taken at the expense of many sacred graves. With increasing acquaintance of the climatic conditions on the Congo the record of losses, previously so fatal to missionary effort, has been less serious lately. The lives of these pioneers have not been wasted. On the fields which they have ploughed and, into which they have thrown the seeds other labourers will stand to gather in the spiritual sheaves. The dust of the Combers— lovingly faithful souls—consecrates African soil afresh to the glory of Christ and His kingdom. They have left no uncertain answer to the question put many years since, " Is England to be a beast of burden or, is she to be an evangelist to all the world?"

Upwards of a score of flourishing stations such as Leopoldville, Nyombe, and Lukelela, on the Lower and Upper Congo, denote the footsteps of English Baptist missionaries, which carry the promise of future developments and conquests. From the base at Leopoldville the work of the Society extends over 900 miles up the river and, to it belongs the honour of having launched in 1882 the first decked steamer on the upper river,—*The Peace*, a gift of Mr. Arthington, Leeds. This historic little craft, not sufficiently large or swift enough for present use has been requisitioned by the Congo Free State. The boiler of the *Peace* was completely fitted up by some of the mission boys and steam raised three days after her construction was commenced. Her successor on the Upper Congo will be the *Goodwill*, a new mission steamer on the twin-screw turbine system, with twice the capacity of her predecessor, being 84 feet long and 13 feet beam, and drawing 2 ft. 2 in. laden with cargo. Each piece of the vessel with hull, boiler, and engine, will be carried on the shoulders of natives some 230 miles over rough hilly roads to her destination at Stanley Pool. The specifications were drawn up by Mr. George Grenfell, the honoured and gifted missionary, who will superintend the building. Welcomed service will be rendered by the *Goodwill* in communicating with the missionaries and stations hundreds of miles apart. In aiding this branch of mission work it is proposed by the Centenary Fund to devote £5,000 for the purchase of a Congo steamer. How faintly are the huge waterways of the Congo apprehended! It is reported that 1,000 miles of its course have never been visited by any missionary and, another 2,000 miles only had a passing glimpse. Facts of this nature demonstrate the need of a missionary flotilla to cruise on these broad, shining waters in the Master's name.

The disappointment that four only of the proposed ten fresh stations have been erected since 1885 is due to the frequent sickness and decease of missionary workers and, in a measure, to the difficulties which beset the missionaries among such a diversity of tribes and strange languages. "They were face to face," said Mr. Grenfell, "with the darkest mass of heathendom the world knew." Keenly were the ambassadors of peace alive to the enormous dimensions of the task before them and prayerfully begged the churches at home to stand by them in sending forth volunteers for the great campaign. The missionaries and explorers knew 6,000 miles of river, or a coast line of 12,000 miles, in Central Africa, the villages and towns along which were all approachable by the missionary. There is intense dismay in Congo missionary organisations that at a time when slave-dealing on the lower stretches of the river is declining another awful evil has been brought in by the white man. Says Mr. Grenfell, " Year by year the infamous liquor traffic was doing more and more to steal from the natives their freedom, and to bring them under a yoke not less terrible than that of slavery. To many of them (the missionaries), it was an open question whether the slave trade was ever a greater curse to the poor African than the liquor traffic was to-day ; a traffic which was reducing him to a wreck, mentally, morally, and physically." The wide-spread effects of drink are so fearful that the missionaries seem well nigh paralysed by its presence and in every direction strenuous endeavours are being made to urge the Powers, and the Congo Free State, to restrict the importation of this abomination into the State, a territory having an area of 1,056,200 square miles and a population of 27,000,000 souls.

In the call to evangelisation, strongly as Mr. Grenfell believes that the leadership and organising qualifications of foreign missionaries are required, he is persuaded that the African nation will not be mainly or ultimately evangelised by whites. He points to an immense region in Central Africa, with an area of 4,000,000 square miles, larger than the whole of Europe, not at present touched by a single missionary and he declares that the heart of the Dark Continent cannot permanently be occupied by white missionaries. The greater part of the work must be done by the natives themselves who happily are showing fitness for the task. Foreign missionaries are less able to grapple with the conditions of native life than African-born agents of whose gifts for carrying spiritual tidings Miss Silvey has penned encouraging testimonies. To the missionaries' appeal for helpers, numbers of the natives, God-fearing men, were nobly responding and freely consecrating themselves that they might win obedience to the faith from their countrymen who, in their turn would bear the light of heaven to the dark regions beyond.

To Mr. Grenfell is allowed the foremost place in the group of English Baptist missionaries on the Congo, in his threefold capacity of pioneer-explorer, leader, and missionary. African geography has been enriched by his notable discovery, that the Mobangi, now proved to be the Welle, flowing from the Central Soudan, is probably the Congo's principal tributary. For this and other explorations he has received the decoration of "Chevalier of the Order of Leopold," from the King of the Belgians, and one of the Royal Geographical Society's gold medals, while his civilising and Christianising labours have been acknowledged in every part of the world. The King of the Belgians holds Mr. Grenfell in high regard, a proof of which is to hand in Mr. Grenfell's acceptance of membership at the King's request, on the Belgian

Commission for the delimitation of the boundary between the Free State and Portuguese territory in the Lunda country. As observed recently by Dr. Maclaren of Manchester, this gallant missionary is one of those who have hazarded their lives for Christianity. In certain quarters there is regret at the proclamation by the King of the Belgians to the Pope, that the Roman Catholic form of Christianity is to be the recognised religion of the Free State, and that His Majesty has placed his African dominions under the direct protection of the Virgin Mary, as the patron saint of the Free State. The announcement does not give the Protestant missionaries any anxiety as they have every facility for missionary aggression and unvarying courtesy from the King's officials.

Of the prevalence of slave-raiding on the upper banks and waters of the Congo, revelations were published similar to those dating from the northern bends of the Niger, the head of Tanganyika, and Bornu. Commander V. Lovett Cameron, a traveller of unquestioned veracity, said, "the part of Africa where this detestable hunting after, murdering, and enslaving human beings was carried on in the worst manner, was the eastern portion of the Congo State." Equally emphatic, and of later date, was the evidence of an independent English trader concerning the same region. Gladly acknowledging that the slave trade on the Lower Congo was dying out with the exception of domestic slavery, he continues, " but in all places of the higher Congo, slavery is being carried on at this present moment. Slavery among the tribes being part and parcel of their social system, they naturally will not part with their custom until they are made to. Slavery is carried on briskly in the cataract regions, between the lower and upper Congo, but certainly, further in the interior the trade is more common, and of larger proportions. As regards the Arabs, it is a very well known fact that they are the most inveterate of all slavers; they are not of the tribes, and therefore have no social system to appeal to as a license. They do not procure slaves for carriers, unless the poor things who are marched in files across country, sometimes for months at a time, can be termed carriers of their own marketable bodies. Yes; in that sense they are carriers." Here, as on the shores of Tanganyika the slave-dealing Arabs are being resisted by Europeans. A message was received in March, 1892, at the offices of the Congo Free State in Brussels, from Captain Ponthier, who has been operating against the Arab slave-raiders guilty of devastating the regions north and south of the Upper Welle. Captain Ponthier met with considerable success, destroying two Arab strongholds. One of these was situated on three small islands some way above the mouth of the Bomokandi, while the other was a fortified camp on the Mokongo. The Arabs had laid waste the whole country with fire and sword, the natives being powerless to oppose them. By Captain Ponthier's forces the Arabs were completely defeated and 250 slaves set at liberty.

The Swedish African explorer, Dr. Westmark, furnished in 1891, thrilling narrations of his explorations on the Upper Congo, amid the cannibal and slave-capturing tribes in Bangalad.

The country itself was a natural paradise, fertile, luxuriant, and of variegated beauty and loveliness, the haunt of :—

> " The mountain wooded to the peak, the lawns
> And winding glades high up like ways to Heaven,
> The slender coco's drooping crown of plumes,
> The lightning flash of insect and of bird,
> The lustre of the long convolvuluses
> That coil'd around the stately stems,"

where man alone was fearfully vile. Slavery flourished there and polygamy is practised. A man can sell wife and children according to his own depraved pleasure. Women are the slave drudges, the men spending their hours in eating, drinking, and sleeping. Cannibalism in its worst features prevails. Young women are prized as special delicacies, particularly girls' ears, prepared in palm-oil and, in order to make the flesh more palatable, the luckless victims are kept in water up to their necks for three or four days before they are slaughtered and served as food. The religious views of these cannibals are extremely crude. Their highest object of adoration is Satan, whom they represent to be white and, to whose glory on great festival occasions cannibalism is perpetrated, in forest-deeps unseen, in tragedies of the most awful and revolting kind.

To check and, finally, to blot out the infamous scourge of slavery in Darkest Africa, the forces of civilised lands and the resources of Christendom are leagued together as in no previous age. The Slave Trade which Pitt long ago called " the greatest practical evil that ever afflicted the human race," is doomed. Commerce, railways, industries, colonisation, barricades, military patrols, blockades, and slave refuges, are severally combating its existence and power. Superior to these in the annihilation of this foe to man, appears the silent ministry of Christianity planting its roots and diffusing its rays over the Congo watershed, across the Soudan, and, in Central Africa. In speeding the daybreak of emancipation on the Congo, and its tributaries, glorious deeds have been wrought by the American Baptist Missionary Union, the Swedish Society, the Congo Balolo Mission, the English Baptists, and, the co-workers with the apostolic William Taylor,

"Missionary Bishop of Africa," whose respective ensigns and missionaries have alleviated sorrow, lessened cruelty, dispelled ignorance, broken slave chains, conquered paganism, and triumphantly uplifted the Cross of Christ.

MISSIONS ON THE NIGER RIVER.

(197)

XI.

MISSIONS ON THE NIGER RIVER.

SPRINGING in the Kong Mountains and coursing northeasterly towards Timbuctoo, and, again, south-southeast-ward, receiving in lat. 7° 40′ N. the Binue, from the sandy depths of the Western Soudan, the Niger,—the second greatest river on the West Coast of Africa,—has an estimated length of 2,500 miles. This imposing waterway empties itself into the Gulf of Guinea by some twenty-two branches which flow through the channelled mangrove-crowned islands of its delta. All the renowned explorers of the Niger, Mungo Park, Caillé, Lander, Allen, Laird, Crowther, and Binger, have described in vivid colours its winding track and charming inland landscapes. Three names designate the divisions of this mighty river: the Niger Delta, the Lower Niger, and the Upper Niger. The lower half of the Niger Delta occupied by thousands of natives runs into the interior fifty miles, with a zigzag coast line, upwards of two hundred miles in length. To the pestilential effluvia rising from fetid mud-banks native life presents a dark counterpart in its enslavement to superstitions, witchcraft, cannibalism, and the white man's firewater. Some rays of light however have been kindled in these malarial haunts and thickets of barbarism whence swarthy-skinned heralds have borne " wonderful words of life" to the inner tribes.

A further ascent of one of the winding channels places the voyager on the bosom of the Niger proper. Gradually the verdure-clad rocky heights which guard the shores are succeeded by low-lying hills and grassy park-land. Differing racial groups inhabit the country. Foremost of these are the Ibos, skilled in the arts of demonology, and next, the Haüsas, a fine bronze-coloured and polished race, fifteen millions in number, who have lately adopted Mohammedan rites. To the north of these races, who are first approached, spread the dominions of the powerful Sultan of Sokoto. Writes an

earnest missionary concerning the Mohammedan states which stretch north and east : " From
vast walled cities of fifty, eighty, even a hundred thousand inhabitants, caravans are always
streaming out—to the south to raid for slaves,
to the north African states across the Sahara
to sell them. Weavers, dyers, and shoemakers
work hard in the streets of these great cities,
manufacturing the ample clothing that the
people wear, and exhibit this remarkable spectacle of African civilisation. From eight degrees latitude to the borders of the Sahara,
and for 3,500 miles from west to east, this vast
region of the Soudan stretches from the Atlantic to the Red Sea, with a population nearly
equal to that of the whole of North America,
under settled rulers, hundreds of thousands
able to read and write, eager to read and re-
read tracts in Arab character till the very paper
is worn to bits. Yet no one has troubled to
send even a few tracts into their great cities."

To evangelise western and north-central
Africa the Church Missionary Society has made
heroic sacrifices and, with its endeavours must

be associated the labours of American societies at Liberia, the Basle Society on the Gold Coast, and the English Wesleyans between Yoruba and the Niger delta. It was in 1816 that the beloved Bickersteth self-denyingly visited the first stations, so that for more than seventy years the Church Missionary Society has continuously, though with chequered episodes, planted the faith by the banks of the Niger.

About 16 years later interest was rekindled in the Niger territory by Lander discovering the mouth of the river and, in 1832 the first Niger Expedition was initiated by Mr. Macgregor Laird, who built the iron paddle steamer, the *Quorra*, which sailed from Liverpool under Captain Lander's command. This gallant man was accompanied by Mr. Laird, Lieut. William Allen, R.N., and other explorers. The expedition had an unhappy experience. Of its complement numbering 40 persons, Mr. Laird and eight others alone returned alive to England. Undismayed, Mr. Laird continued to be an ardent worker for the exploration of the Niger by fitting out repeated expeditions and equipping the steamers. In 1841 an expedition was dispatched by the British Government for which Mr. John Laird, the founder of the eminent shipbuilding firm, equipped the *Albert*, *Wilberforce*, and the *Soudan*. With this venture the ardently consecrated Rev. J. F. Schön, of Sierra Leone, and a young African named Samuel Crowther, whose previous history was as romantic as his subsequent one was distinguished in missionary annals, were identified. The crews were stricken with fever and, of 150 whites 42 died. From this expedition the missionaries had an opportunity of learning that some of the native tribes were willing to receive Gospel teachings. A further expedition had a disastrous issue, followed by another one in 1854, both of which Crowther joined. The last of these noted expeditions sailed in 1857, which marks the definite establishment of the Niger Mission.

The life of the first Bishop of the Niger and the only coloured non-European bishop consecrated in England since the apostolic age, is too fascinating to be excluded from a brief narration. Thrown into slavery in youth by Eyo Mohammedans the boy Adjai suffered terribly and was afterwards shipped with a living cargo of fellow-victims from the African coast for western shores. Rescued by a British man-of-war in 1822 he was landed at Bathurst, near Free Town, and there receiving a good education was next transferred to a mission at Free Town. In 1825 he was baptised into the Christian religion and the names—Samuel Crowther, after an eminent London Evangelical clergyman, adopted. A hurried visit to England was followed by recommencing study at Fourah Bay College. He returned again to Great Britain and on the completion of extensive studies was ordained in 1843 for missionary service at Yoruba and Sierra Leone by the Bishop of London. The same year he founded in conjunction with Mr. Townsend and Mr. Gollmer the Yoruba Mission, to which he devoted himself passionately for upwards of twelve years. In 1846 he met once more his long lost mother and had the additional joy of ransoming at the same time several of his kindred from slave fetters. Returning from the Niger Expedition of 1854 he led for two years the Lagos Mission, which was sent up the river in 1857; and, in 1864, the supreme devotedness of this master missionary was recognised by his consecration in Canterbury Cathedral to the Niger Bishopric. In the busiest and most active of his years he toiled incessantly in translating portions of the Bible, religious works, and other kinds of literature into the native tongues and dialects. His farewell departure from Liverpool in February, 1890, in his eighty-second year, with a band of fellow-labourers, was a memorable incident, opening afresh the vision of missionary possibilities in a sphere of trying vicissitudes. Nearly two years later, on the 31st of December, 1891, the good Bishop, a Shepherd of God's flock, went into the glory with a doubtless abundant entrance and followed by the praises of thousands of God's people on many shores.

A few weeks afterwards a telegram was received, dated March 19, from Brass, by the Church Missionary Society announcing in a

brief sentence the death of Mr. Graham Wilmot Brooke, the young, trusted, capable, and
devoted leader of the Mission on the Upper
Niger:—

"Wilmot Brooke at rest—March 5—black-
water fever."

By the same severe malady had been carried
off some months earlier, Mr. J. A. Robinson, a
gifted Cambridge colleague.

The spiritual emancipation of the Mohammedans occupying the Central Soudan was the
master passion of Mr. Brooke,—a true martyr-
missionary:—

> " Wearing the light yoke of that Lord of love,
> Who still'd the rolling wave of Galilee."

In his earlier essays to reach these millions
he ventured on apostolic lines partly sustained by the generosity of friends at home.
It was in the course of his third perilous journey that he was detained upwards of four
months on the Mobangi, a northern tributary
of the Congo, and hemmed in for hundreds
of miles by the most savage tribes. Having
grandly failed on these occasions to break

through the barriers of the impenetrable Soudan from the south, he laid his scheme before the Church Missionary Society in England. The proposals were approved and Mr. Brooke's transference to the Society's staff in 1890, was ratified with the heartiest concurrence of his former helpers and patrons. Again he travelled eastward along the Lower and Upper Niger to enter the Western Soudan, passing through the territories of sultans and emirs who scorned the Christian faith. For protection against the Mohammedan law which threatens with death the proselytizer and proselytized, Mr. Brooke and his brother evangelists had none save the divine arm. Electing to stand on the convert's level in his profession of allegiance to Jesus his much loved Master and Lord, Graham Wilmot Brooke died, carrying the loftiest traditions of missionary courage.

Not on any other field of high enterprise perhaps has the Church Missionary Society realised so much of severe conflict, crucial struggle, and travail in pioneership as in the series of Niger campaigns. Upon every page of its story shadows fall. Significantly has it been remarked that the Niger River has always been a source of material or spiritual disaster to the Society's directors. What savagery and barbarism have reigned over these West African lands for generations! There the most devilish forms of cruelty known to humanity flourish to-day. Fierce tribal warfare, human butcheries, the endless passage of canoe loads of slaves on tributary waters consigned as the food of cannibal tribes, revolting sacrifices, and rank degradation, have appalled the most intrepid of the missionary vanguard. The more welcome are the signs that darkness does not entirely prevail. Groups of converts and centres of faith have existence in these regions of heathenism. Report tells of the native Christians at Bonny on the coast holding forth the word of life. Where in past years, during their trading expeditions for palm oil and palm kernel, sixty miles distant, at the Ura Ya markets, they assembled in rough praying sheds in the heart of heathen villages the same fervid light-

bearers now gather on the identical site in com-
modious and neatly-erected timber chapels. At
the village of Okrika, a few miles from Bonny, the
cause of evangelisation was making way when in
the autumn of 1889 a deplorable outbreak of cannibalism practically ruined the hopeful prospects.
In one day, the heathen, and several village
Christians, under a tribal passion, cooked and devoured a hundred and twenty prisoners of war.

Onitsha, situated in a pleasant and fertile lo-
cality on the Lower Niger, is the seat of vigorous missionary aggression whither the Haüsas,
Nupés, Igbirras, and Igarras, bring their produce. The Igbirras and Basas have shown
unfaltering courage in defying the charges of
Moslem invaders through long decades. Looking easterly the Fulanis are seen, governed
by Ahmadu, Sultan of Sequ Sikoro, of inferior civilisation to the Haüsas, and in whom
the Gospel will have a strong antagonist.
Opposite Onitsha lies Asaba, the headquarters
of the Niger territory, and many miles up
the river, the town of Ghebe, below the
confluence of the Binue and Niger, which

constitutes the southernmost branch of the
Soudan division of the Niger Mission. Some
miles beyond the inflowing mouth of the Binue
stands the notable town of Lokoja with 3,000
inhabitants at the foot of one of the numerous
table mountains. Lokoja, the base of the Society's interior offshoots, three hundred miles
from the coast, in which a hospital will be
opened, has a future of promising usefulness,
in advancing the spread of missions. To the
north of it, Egga, a town of larger population,
is another growing station where the " mal-
lams," or, African Mohammedan scribes, assemble every Friday, to preach Islamite doctrines to groups of semi-barbarian listeners.

Ere the traveller touches these extreme out-
posts he sees the relics of awful tragedies in
the intermediate districts from which the cries
of the victims are unheard within the bounds
of civilisation. At Azumiri, the skulls of natives, killed and eaten in sacrifice to the gods,
are strung up by hundreds in the open streets,
to be gazed upon and worshipped by defenceless innocents whose fate may be decreed on

the following day. Of dark Ohambele and its slaughters at burial ceremonials Bishop Crowther related a tragical occurrence. " About four days before our arrival at Ohambele an old rich woman was dead and buried. When the grave was dug, two female slaves were taken, whose limbs were smashed with clubs. Being unable to stir, they were let down into the grave, yet alive, on mat or bed on which the corpse of the mistress was laid, and screened from sight for a time. Two other female slaves were laid hold of and dressed up with best clothes and coral beads. This being done, they were led and paraded about the town to show the public the servants of the rich dead mistress, whom they would attend in the world of spirits. This was done for two days, when the unfortunate victims were taken to the edge of the grave, and their limbs were also smashed with clubs, and their bodies laid on the corpse of their mistress and covered up with earth while yet alive. Some of the Bonny converts attempted to rescue these last two females by a large offer of ransom to buy bullocks for the occasion, but it was refused them." These dreadful and frequently enacted crimes against humanity must evoke the supplication from the children of God, " How long, O Lord, how long ?" coupled with an unshaken resolve that such deeds shall be effectually blotted out from the face of the whole earth.

With the death of Bishop Crowther, the last of the great pioneers of Christianity on the Niger watershed and, in Western Africa, has been gathered home. It is naturally regretted that the declining years of the veteran whose labours had been exceedingly fruitful, should have suffered disappointment from the alleged spiritual weakness of some of the converts or, the lack of qualification on the part of native African agents. There is every anticipation that the visit of a deputation consisting of Archdeacon Hamilton and the Rev. W. Allan to the Niger province in 1891 will heal the disputes and misunderstandings. The obstacles overcome the messengers of the Cross will again speed the Word :—

" Till the sunrise broad of the day of God
    Shall shine on the victor's glory,
    And the earth at rest, in her Lord confessed,
    Shall rejoice in the finished story."

The question of a successor to Bishop Crowther, the black bishop of the Niger, is of moment to the missionary enterprise in that region. In a growing measure the view prevails in church missionary circles that a native, on account of the likelihood of his standing the climate better, and, even for weightier reasons, should have the appointment. This view being adopted the claims of the Rev. Isaac Oluwole, a graduate of Durban University, and one of the native clergy will probably receive recognition for recommendation to the Archbishop of Canterbury.

Crowns of light encircle the names of Raban, Haensel, Schön, Robinson, Crowther, and Brooke. These servants of God scorned to lay sandy foundations which would not endure in the day when every man's work shall be tested and its reward determined. What steadfast toilers they were in surveys of evangelisation, in winning native confidence, in establishing stations, in caring for the young, in translating literature, and, in shaping a line of civilisation by means of which later generations of tribes may be redeemed from the gloom of barbarism ! Nor should the services of the Royal Niger Company, previously called the National African Company, and, antecedently, the United African Company, Limited, be forgotten. Agreeable to the Company's charter the gin trade is rigorously excluded from the sphere of its jurisdiction. Though it fulfils a rôle on the Niger similar to the old East India Company in levying duties, keeping soldiers, building forts, and exercising administrative functions, the Company's officers have aided missions, carried the missionaries and their freight, guarded their settlements, and, in unrecorded ways removed hindrances from the pathway of missionary progress.

A ROMANCE OF THE EQUATORIAL SOUDAN.

XII.

A ROMANCE OF THE EQUATORIAL SOUDAN.

By the arrival of three missionary fugitives, Father Ohrwalder, and the Sisters Catherina Chincarini and Elizabetta Venturini at Cairo, on the 21st of December, 1891, another picture has been supplied of the soul-thrilling events connected with the Soudan. These long-suffering captives overjoyed at their escape from the grasp of a savage tyrant could scarcely realise that they were free with the prospect of seeing once more their native land. Their capture, and all its consequent hardships, tortures, and embittered imprisonment, from which release by death must often have seemed preferable, furnishes an extraordinary narrative.

Under the auspices of the Austrian Roman Catholic Mission to the Soudan, the refugees left Cairo eleven years back. As early as 1882, the two mission locations at El-Obeid and, at Jebel-Gedir,—three days' journey distant, were doing admirable work in training dusky liberated slaves in various trades and in the art of agriculture. That year the revolt of the Mahdi burst forth and, following the "holy flag" Emir El Nejumi, a remarkable Soudanese figure, shattered Hicks Pacha's army and seized Khartoum. The little mission stations, quite isolated, were placed on the defensive and, for months, heroically sustained a siege, and only yielded when the black troops betrayed them and their own staff was reduced by sickness, exposure, and death. With the termination of the siege at El-Obeid in January, 1883, the two priests terribly exhausted and emaciated in body, made a profession of Islamism, the nuns, meanwhile obstinately refusing every entreaty. During the ensuing fifteen months these five brave women were locked up, in harsh confinement, in a house at El-Obeid, and never once throughout that time were they allowed to cross the threshold. Cut off from the least gleam of comfort and chance of deliverance, their fate,—a life of death, was of the most melancholy character. A fresh effort was made by the Khalifa Abdullah in March, 1884, to secure the conversion to Mohammedanism, of the seven priests taken from Jebel-Gedir. Tempting inducements and fierce threats were vain, and upon their being ordered to send the nuns, they chivalrously answered that the Moslem law forbade women to stand in the presence of strangers. Thus foiled, the Khalifa had the sisters placed before himself for trial. That ordeal each of them firmly withstood, whereupon they were banished separately as domestic slaves of the soldiers, the priests filling a similar office. No chronicler will ever narrate the sufferings of the nuns at this period or, the barbarities to which these gentle and defenceless women were subjected. The inhuman captors slit the nose of Teresa Grigolini and flogged Sister Venturini tied, standing to a tree. They were afterwards driven on foot almost naked to Rabat, to face the Mahdi, and, in despair, they embraced Mohammedanism to escape worse tortures. The departure, subsequently, of Sisters Chincarini and Venturini, from Omdurman, situate in :—

"the long desert in the south,"

left Sister Teresa Grigolini, the last of the nuns, lingering there alone in captivity.

Throughout the eight years of bondage Father Ohrwalder speaks of their agonies being at times unbearable. Even in sickness and lying for days entirely prostrate, they were denied the necessaries of life. Upon the Sisters the Mahdi especially inflicted shameful cruelties, and, unaware of the destruction of Khartoum, the captives, for a while, had hopes of relief from that quarter. In 1882 they received the latest news concerning the outside world from an Arabic newspaper, which announced the bombardment of Alexandria. After that they saw neither book nor paper of any description and, gradually, their expectation of again enjoying liberty vanished. For their subsistence the Mahdi made no provision. His rule was to allow them a few hours of release each day in order to earn a living, in the best way possible and, latterly, Father Ohrwalder eked out a trifle of piastres daily, by tailoring and cloth-weaving, the Sisters occupying themselves with baking and selling bread, in and around Omdurman, for an existence. The sovereignty of the Mahdi, and that of his successor, the Khalifa, frequently presented scenes of unexampled savagery. Through two dark and weary years something too was seen of the horrors of famine, the ravages of small-pox and typhus fever, which desolated a wide area of the inner Soudan. The privileges of the prisoners were of a meagre order, in illustration of which it is noted that eighteen months before quitting their land of confinement, they were granted the luxury of dwelling in mud huts, in exchange for shelters made of cane and maize stalks, reared by their own hands.

In a hazardously and romantic fashion Father Ohrwalder and the Sisters Chincarini and Venturini, managed to gain their freedom. This daring step was attempted on November 29, 1891, at the height of a struggle between

some Danagla Khalifas and, the Khalifa, Abdullah Baggara, semi-savage tribesmen, in which
17 of the latter and 7 of the former, perished.
A black female slave who waited upon them
ingeniously planned the line of flight. This
tender-hearted and compassionate native, obtained the camels, fixed the hour, and chose
the route of their exodus. Lest the slave
might be forced to give information of the
departure, if left behind, the travellers pre-
vailed upon her to accompany them. At the
outset of this perilous race for life the Sisters
wore Arab female costumes while the Father
dressed himself as a trader. Early joined by
three friendly Arab camel-drivers, they all pursued their way day and night, without any
stoppage, except for a couple of days, at the
Murad Wells. For three days they had no
food. So great was their dread of recapture,
that sleep on the road was impossible and, on
one occasion, Sister Venturini, overcome by
exhaustion, fell from her camel. At the ex-
piration of nine days, having travelled 550
miles from Omdurman, they safely arrived at

Korosko, on the Nile, to the north of Wady
Halfa. They were much impressed with the
hearty reception accorded them at Korosko,
and, after a brief halt, the refugees, at the invitation of the Government of the late Khedive,
went northward, by Assouan, to Cairo. In physique, Father Ohrwalder was tall and thin, and
apparently about 40 years of age. The Sisters,
bearing traces of painful suffering, were vigorous, in spite of what they had endured in the
length of a nine years' captivity. A priest, a
lay brother, and Sister Teresa Grigolini, at Omdurman, are the surviving members of the ill-
fated mission.

An interesting coincidence touching the released lady prisoners is found in a recent pub-
lication descriptive of Gessi Pacha's " *Seven
Years in the Soudan.*" In an appendix reference is made to the Italian Mission, in 1881,
some of whose members tended Gessi in his
illness at Khartoum. The passage reads :—
" The Sisters of the Italian Mission, whose
names we will record because they afterwards
fell into the hands of the Mahdi, nursed Gessi

by turns, giving a good example of the highest Christian virtue." Last in this roll of eleven heroic women stand the names of "Caterina Chincarini and Elisa Venturini." A later volume entitled, "*Mahdiism and the Egyptian Soudan*," reviewing the changes in the far Soudan, thus introduces a list of the captives :— " Of the Austrian Mission (most of whom are Italians), there are now, it is said, at Omdurman," (which is reached by a ferry across the White Nile from Khartoum), "Father Don Guiseppe Ohrwalder, whose Arabic name is Yusef." In the same group the two Sisters cited above are mentioned, and also, " Sisters Teresa Grigolini and Concetto Corsi." Of the remaining captives detained in 1891, at Omdurman, whose names recall the painful events of 1883, there were 19 Greeks, 8 Syrians, 8 Jews, the German merchant Neufeldt, heavily chained, who was captured in 1884, while acting as interpreter to the British forces, and, Slatin Bey, all of them leading an existence of misery, though in tolerable health. Perhaps something may yet be gleaned of the fate of Lupton, who had never left the Soudan since Gordon's first expedition. Neufeldt was popular in Cairo,—a good colloquial Arabic scholar, with previous experiences of the Soudan. The lot of Slatin Bey opens again the story of a romantic career. Formerly Governor-General of Darfur, and a man of intrepid heart, he fought 27 battles in defence of his province before surrendering to the Mahdi's nominee,—following the defeat of Hicks Pacha's column. He accompanied Mohammed Ahmed to Khartoum, saw with his own eyes, its downfall, and, on the Mahdi's death, was made one of the Khalifa's Mulazimin, or, body-guard. Invariably in attendance on the Khalifa, the movements of Slatin, who was accustomed to stand in the outer courtyard, were quickly and closely noticed by his master from within the halls of the palace.

Of the great Soudan, which Sir Samuel Baker still holds, may, under a just rule, become one of the most fruitful countries in the world, notably, as a source of cotton supply, the refugees brought the latest reliable tidings.

Omdurman was a strong city, of no mean celebrity with many stone houses and a population of about 150,000 inhabitants, consisting of a mixture of all the tribes in the Soudan. With the Khalifa Abdullah, are the Khalifs, Ali El-Faruch and Ali El-Karer or El-Sherif. Other personages of importance there include Jakub, the brother and factotum of Abdullah, and Jadi Ahmed and Nur-el-Gerefani, and the treasurer, Bet-el-mal. Upwards of two thousand slaves represent the Abdullah's troops. When the three missionary captives were fleeing they espied at a lonely spot, called Esaa, two days' journey south of Khartoum, the burial-place of Olivier Pain, who, it seems, falling from his camel, through sickness, was captured. His body lies below a few inches of sand. Except in Kordofan food was cheap and usually plentiful over the Soudan, where most of the well-meaning tribes would welcome the return of a stable, Egyptian sway. Despite the Khalifa's numerous following the majority of these were only slightly attached to him personally which gave weight to Father Ohr-

walder's opinion that, in the endlessly, disturbed state of affairs, a small force might
easily re-conquer much of the Soudan, save it
from ruin, and the waste of years of patriotic
labours which a succession of distinguished
men have given for its reclamation. Darfur
is deserted. Kordofan is occupied by Emir
Mahmud Ahmed and Emir Abd-el-Bogi,—relations of Abdullah ; who, at El-Obeid, have fifteen hundred soldiers. On the White Nile, the
posts are Djebel-Red-giaf, Lado, and Fashoda ;
Emir Zeki Tamal, ruling at the latter place,
with nearly six thousand men. In Sennaar,
the most advanced post is Karkoe, and at Gala-
bet, Emir Mohammed Ali, has a fortified one.
At Kassala, some five hundred men are armed
with guns, and, at Berber, Emir Zeki rules,
and Yunez, at Dongola. The two last named
positions abandoned a few years ago by the
British, are regarded as the keys of that portion
of the Soudan which commands the Nile between Khartoum and Assouan. As the great
centres of the Soudan trade and the granaries
of the country they are of prime concern to

merchants and the commercial world.   Khartoum,—the city of the heroic General Gordon,
that "soldier-priest," of whom the nations have
said with one acclaim :—

> "A man more pure and bold and just
> Was never born into the earth ;"—

is forsaken.   Weeds grow over its ruins.   The
sites of the houses are covered with vegetation.
Only the gardens, the Austrian Church, and
Gordon's palace, all in decay, are seen in deso-
late Khartoum.

Faint hopes remain of freeing the 40, or more
Europeans, in the clutch of the Khalifa Abdullah, at Omdurman, save through the success of
the rescue expedition to be headed by three
European officers in the autumn of 1892.
Beneath the shadow of the unscrupulous, igno-
rant, oppressing, and cruel Abdullah, whose
professed subjects would gladly hail relief from
his tyranny, the lives of the captives are drea-
rily wasting away.   The territory vaguely de-
fined by the term, "Soudan," is of immense
extent, with an area nearly equal to that of
India, embracing a million and a half square

miles, peopled by races, eleven millions in number, and, of wide diversities in speech, characteristics, physiognomy, and tribal antagonisms.
The Soudanese native population which thirty
years ago was constantly diminishing by in-
ternal and desperate feuds, and exportations to
the slave markets at Cairo and Mecca, has
latterly been steadily increasing. By the gar-
risons of the Egyptian Government, weak and
corrupt in many respects, a reign of order was
partially established and, a decisive check given
to slave-bartering, the beneficial effects of which
are felt at the present hour on the population.
For these multiplying hordes the produce of
the soil is becoming insufficient and, consequently, the hardier and more adventurous
tribes are migrating in search of fresh territories and empire beyond. This so-called
"flood of barbarism" trending on the confines
of Upper Egypt cannot be unaffected by the
enlightening rule which is transfiguring the
civil life of Egypt and ushering in an epoch of
national prosperity.

Over Egypt, the "gift of the Nile," the

gateway to the burning Soudan, the sky is brightening. Egypt's finances, legislation, and material status, indicate that she is beginning to march with the nations. A modified taxation, a rise in land values, an expanding export trade, and, a growing revenue, are some of the first-fruits of a humane and masterly administration. The old native executive wherein a certain type of provincial governor had un-questioned license was wrong in principle, prolific in abominations, and utterly demoralising. This system based on extortion and the lash has disappeared. A new era has dawned. Sir Evelyn Baring and his brilliant staff have inaugurated the initial stages of a healthy civilisation. They have swept abuses aside and energetically laboured for future reforms. The training of superior natives for official posts has been kept to the forefront and thus in a short time the dearth of capable young Egyptians will be met by the spread of educational advantages and, familiarity with European ideas and forms of government. For triumphs in extensive drainage and irrigation the year

1891 in the annals of Egypt, under the British régime, will have historic mark. The most sanguine predictions respecting the barrage works were surpassed, the cotton crop being larger than any of previous years. In accomplishing this scheme three steps were adopted ; the waters of the Nile were gathered, thence distributed into capacious channels, and, lastly, sound precautions taken that the poorer natives should not be exploited by their richer neighbours. It is not improbable that in a few years the flood-waters of the ancient Nile may be caught in gigantic reservoirs in Upper Egypt, and, by this means, areas of land in the lower districts receive supplies of the precious liquid during the hot season. For these engineering achievements in operation and in prospect, the Egyptian peasant is as much a debtor to the genius of Sir Colin Moncrieff, as he is in civil and military affairs, to Colonel Kitchener's zeal, ability, and jurisdiction.

With the sway of a progressive Government in Egypt Proper whether directed by European Powers or subject to the independent rule of

His Highness, the young Khedive, Abbas Pasha Helmy, the stream of life and of modern civilisation must flow southwards to the desert tribes who have their home in the Eastern Soudan. In that sphere of the Dark Continent weird and fascinating historical dramas have figured, where Ethiopian, Egyptian, Persian, Roman, Grecian, Saracen, and Turkish waves of conquest have successively rolled and vanished, leaving faint traces of their sovereign dynasties. Gazing east and west from the foliaged and castle-studded banks of the Upper Nile over hundreds of miles of arable tracts and Saharan wastes of yellow sand a mass of heathenism—deep, awful, and profound—has its habitation, unbroken by a single beam of divine light. Afar off on the horizon northward, the dawn of an early morning sunlight glimmers. To the natives of the wide-spreading Soudan, the North Africa Mission, the Church Missionary Society, and the Central Soudan Mission in Tripoli, are turning their thoughts and energies. "Truth shall spring out of the earth"; and, in ransoming Soudanese Ethiopians, Be-

douins, Nubæ, and Berberines, the American
missionaries on the Nile and their British col-
leagues in the Dependency of Tripoli promise
to become the heralds of Christ in evangelising
races lying in the region of the shadow of
death for whose resurrection these ensigns not
unhopefully sing :—

" O'er the realms of night, shall our standard bright
　　Arise, their darkness clearing ;
　And the souls that were dead to the Lord who bled,
　　Shall revive at His glad appearing."

ON THE BANKS OF LAKE
TANGANYIKA.

XIII.

ON THE BANKS OF LAKE TANGANYIKA.

IN that wonderful lake system which formed a chain of communication, north and south, through the interior of Africa, Lake Tanganyika occupied a central place. The most westerly of the great inland waters, it has Victoria Nyanza to the north-east and, Lake Nyasa, for its south-eastern neighbour. These immense lakes, the reservoirs of thousands of rivers, were destined as soon as navigation by steamer was possible to exercise a civilising influence on the savage tribes which frequented their shores. With a magnificent shore line of 363 miles, Tanganyika is now recognised as the western boundary of the German sphere of territory in East Central Africa, adjoining which was the fertile and picturesque State of Usibi and

Wanga described by Stanley as certainly "to turn out one of the most unique regions in Africa." The discovery of Lake Tanganyika was made before the real sources of the Nile had been determined and at a period less than forty years ago when a pall of darkness lay over most of the countries of Central Africa. Never perhaps in the records of exploration have two travellers returned to the haunts of civilisation each of whom could claim such marvellous "finds" as had fallen to the lot of Burton and Speke on emerging in 1859 from the African wilds. Captain Richard Burton held in his possession the discovery of Tanganyika and, his comrade Speke,—Lake Ukerewe, which he named Victoria Nyanza, and rightly concluded to be the origin and head of Father Nile. The geographical areas of Tanganyika show that it stands 2,756 feet above the sea level with a superficial area of 9,240 square miles and encircling this grand stretch of water rise a series of noble, forest-crowned heights which afford views of enchanting beauty :—

"fair
As ever painter painted, poet sang,
Or Heav'n in lavish bounty moulded."

The usual route to Lake Tanganyika has been overland, a distance of 830 miles from Zanzibar, viâ Mpwapwa, Unyanyembe, Urambo, to Ujiji, the chief mart of the Lake, situated on the north-easterly shore. To make the journey along the rough, zig-zag foot and wagon track required about 100 days, a tedious line of march, which was practically abandoned in 1891 by the Directors of the London Missionary Society, for the safer, easier, and more direct approach which is afforded by sailing up the Zambesi, Shiré, across Lake Nyasa, and over the valued missionary highway,—the Stevenson Road, uniting the north-end of Nyasa and the southern point of Tanganyika. Around the Lake swarm some dozen independent tribal races whose villages, market places, and trading depôts present animated native-life pictures. Every part of the Lake shores is visited by merchants and representatives of motley races and people,—Portuguese from the west coast, Arabs from Zanzibar, Swahili, Wasagara, Wakaguru, the half-naked, repulsive Wagogo, the Wahumba and Wakimbu, and the all-pervading Wanyamwezi. On the sunny surface of Tanganyika craft of every pattern glide to and fro. The ordinary canoe has the shape of that ungainly animal—one of Africa's well known denizens—the hippopotamus, and hewn out of the massive trunk of a forest king. Roughly finished it is launched on the Lake, the native piloting it, indifferent to the possibility of danger, with surprising dexterity. Scores of these canoes may be seen in a starry night on the bosom of the Lake, their occupants engaged in whitebait fishing. By placing a bundle of blazing dried reeds at the bow of the vessel thousands of these fish are attracted and easily caught in the large hand-net which the native holds. After drying the "catches" on shore in a tropic sun they are packed in leaves and sent to far away tribes. Natives visiting the shore-markets introduce the utmost variety of manufacture and produce: skins, woven cotton cloth, mats, baskets, pottery, wire, iron hoes and axes, weapons, copper in the rough and artistically designed in the form of bracelets and ingeniously made ornaments; supplemented with ground nuts, sugar cane, honey, butter, salt, palm oil, fish, goats, fowls, and vegetables. The myriads of native people are hard-working and full of clever resource. Larger canoes, 40 or more feet long, are used for traffic on an extensive scale, notoriously in the shipment of slaves, between the races inhabiting different points on the shore. Practised universally this hideous scourge has retarded for generations the progress of the numerous tribes. Physically, the natives are strong, handsomely-built, and capable of great endurance. At the extreme north end—a densely populated region—the people are fine in appearance, manly, intelligent, and well-disposed save for an irrepressible tendency to treachery. In 1890 they were visited by Mr. Swann and previous to his landing in their midst, they had not hitherto had any communication whatever with white faces. Were the London Missionary Society in possession of larger reinforcements the district offers a broad field for pioneering labours. Native character on Tanganyika, typical of the whole of the Central African tribes, was negative. They were destitute of the spirit of true self-reliance and the higher virtues, the maxim of traders and travellers in dealing with them was, if the natives do not fear the white man, the white man feared them, followed by incessant troubles and disaster.

Missionary work by the London Society on the banks of Lake Tanganyika actually dates from the spring of 1874, when the London papers printed that mournful telegram: " Livingstone is really dead, and his body is coming home in one of the Queen's ships." English Christians were intensely stirred and, in three years' time the London Missionary Society at Tanganyika, the Church Missionary Society in Uganda, and the Livingstonia Mission in Nyasa-land, were devotedly bending their energies for the redemption of Africa's children from the woes of slavery and heathenism. Livingstone's words: " Go forward, and with the

Divine blessing you will surely succeed. Do
you carry on the work which I have begun. I
leave it with you "; were trumpet calls to which
volunteers, men of resolution,—an advanced
guard, made answer. Heroes indeed, believing
that the Africans were :—

"Not past the living fount of pity in Heaven."

That high level of ardour which the leaders
of the Central African Mission exhibited has
been emulated by their train of successors.
The "coinage true" of these pioneers was in-
trepidity, valour, fortitude, and inextinguish-
able enthusiasm, and, alas, upon their thin
ranks the fatal enemy fell with terrible might.
First of the martyr-band was the Rev. J. B.
Thomson, fellow-traveller of Captain Hore and
Mr. Hutley, the earliest missionary arrivals
at Tanganyika. Standing on the immediate
threshold of his task Mr. Thomson's death
is a pathetic story. After the exhausting
march of more than 800 miles to Ujiji he
had visited with the others the site for a proposed temporary station on a hill overlooking

the lovely Kigoma Bay, and, a month later, on Sunday afternoon, September 22, 1878, he died, and soon afterwards was laid to rest on the spot by his sorrowing companions—his own dust consecrating the place and enterprise. Year by year deaths were of constant occurrence including that great-hearted man Dr. Mullens, who was cut down in the early days of the mission and buried at Mpwapwa, and the beloved Dr. Southon (U. S. A.), the tragic close of whose career in 1882, sent a thrill of regret far over the Christian world. During the ensuing ten years, one relay after another was decimated until it was doubted by the supporters whether God had not raised a barrier against white men inhabiting these fever-haunted lands. So fearful was the harvest of fatality that not one of the names found on the Central African Mission staff in 1881 appears on that of 1891. The conjecture might be made that "God saw fit to take them into *life*, and, may be, their vision of events on earth to-day is clearer, and so more hopeful." These nights of sorrow and blighted prospects have been succeeded by the dawn of brighter days and, in the years from 1888 to 1891 no death was reported due to the unhealthiness of the climate.

Than the history of the Central African Mission few chapters in the annals of the infancy of missions have been as chequered or furnished such vivid illustrations of repeated and vain endeavours to establish a foothold. From the month of August, 1878, when Captain Hore and his cavalcade of 225 men in single file, each with his load on head or shoulder, led by Songoro, bearing the Union Jack with snowy border and, in the centre of this strange procession Juma Mackay, displaying on a long bamboo, the dove of peace with olive branch, wound through the Ujiji plantation gardens of plantains, palms, beans, maize, and potatoes and after a long ascent to the heights above Ujiji which allowed a view of the glorious Tanganyika beyond, the missionaries have strenuously and heroically battled in the face of adverse circumstances. In its operations Captain Hore's career has been one of distinguished service. At the outset he took up his residence near Ujiji and subsequently made, first in a native canoe, thousands of trips into various parts of the Lake bays and gulfs, to prepare the way for enabling the messengers of the Gospel to reach the remotest homes of heathen communities and there proclaim a knowledge of the " White Man's God." Making the acquaintance of the principal chiefs and their subjects and carefully surveying and mapping out portions of the boundaries of Lake Tanganyika which had not been investigated previously by Livingstone, Cameron, or Stanley, he then returned to England with a design for the steel life-boat, to be known as *Nyota ya Assubui—The Morning Star.* This craft 32 feet long and 8 feet beam was shipped from London to Zanzibar, conveyed in sections by native carriers to Ujiji, built by Captain Hore, with the aid of the natives, and launched amid wild rejoicings in May, 1883. At an earlier period the mission sustained a severe blow by the death of Mr. A. W. Dodgshun,— a faithful standard-bearer ; and, meanwhile settlements were effected at Unyamwezi, Uguha, and Ujiji. A cheering outlook was presented in 1880 which unfortunately was doomed to a second series of disappointments. In 1881–2 a complete dispersion occurred. Mr. Wookey and Dr. Palmer went home invalided, Mr. Williams was carried off by sunstroke, and Mr. Hutley left, shattered in health. Two stations, 300 miles apart, were then held respectively by Mr. Griffiths and Dr. Southon. A large party of missionaries arrived at Zanzibar in June, 1882, whose plans were altered considerably by the painful news of Dr. Southon's decease. In the course of its advance inland, Mr. Dineen died at the new station of Uguha, and Mr. Penry suffering from the long marches was seized with dysentery at Urambo, where he was unwillingly obliged to turn homewards. Death overtook him near Mpwapwa, his remains being there interred by the side of the late Dr. Mullens. The health of Mr. Willoughby giving way he returned immediately to England and the band, sadly weakened, reached Ujiji ten months from the date of leaving London. Another loss came in 1884, Mr. Dunn dying from fever, after a few days' illness. The same year Captain Hore made an adventurous journey through Nyasa-land to Quillimane and, in January, 1885, brought a fresh company of missionaries viâ Zanzibar.

It was now decided to remove the head-quarters of the marine department from Ujiji to Kavala, an island opposite to Uguha, ruled over by Kassanga. The new steamer, the *Good News* (although not finished) was floated on Tanganyika, in 1885 by Mr. Roxburgh, a practical engineer. After bringing her safely to Kavala, this ardent worker, to the sorrow of all, died of fever and dysentery. A little later Mr. Harris was fatally stricken, and the building at the south end consequently abandoned. That same year Messrs. Jones and Rees worn out with fatigue and recurring fever attacks relinquished their posts and, inevitably, Uguha was vacated. The year 1886 opened by the arrival at Kavala of Mr. Carson, an engineer, who completed the fitting up of the steamer. So slowly had the fittings come to hand that three years elapsed—a time of no small strain to those concerned—ere the *Good News* had her finishing touches. The lamentable experience of the mission showing that in deaths and retirements three men on an average had been lost yearly, caused the directors to recommend their missionaries in 1887 to erect a settlement at Fwambo, a reputed healthy spot, at considerable elevation. During 1887 Mr. Lea and Dr. Tomory retired and, towards the end of the year Fwambo was temporarily forsaken by the missionaries, with the exception of the Rev. D. P. Jones, owing to the war which had broken out south-eastwards between the half-caste Arabs and the Europeans, at Karonga. In 1888 Captain and Mrs. Hore returned to England and Mr. Swann, accompanying another contingent of missionaries, was appointed Captain Hore's successor in superintending the marine department at Kavala. The mission at the close of 1888 had a sore bereavement. Mr. Brooks, an esteemed co-worker journeying to the coast to enjoy a well-earned holiday, was brutally murdered by some East Coast Arabs;

the poor fellow it is surmised was mistakenly identified with the Germans, the adversaries of the Arabs at that period. Agreeable to home instructions Messrs. Swann and Carson next fixed upon Kinyamkolo as a suitable harbour and new marine headquarters at the south-end of the Lake, which would further enable the missionaries in the vicinity to have ready access to Fwambo for health sojourns. Throughout 1889–90 the missionaries were shut off from the civilised world. For a year they had no home letters and were without European provisions except those which the African Lakes Company kindly conveyed. At the end of this isolation, if not siege, Mr. Wright, disabled by sickness was obliged to leave the field. Subsequently the mission with a staff of nine missionaries, doctors, artisan auxiliaries, and missionaries' wives preserved from a repetition of many of its calamities in bygone years has the promise of expansion and fruitfulness.

At Urambo, Kinyamkolo, and Fwambo, the native languages are being mastered, first translations made, schools opened, Sunday services

conducted, and domestic and industrial training provided. If these are not on an extensive
scale or systematic in form the peculiarities of
the situation are responsible. Commenting on
this feature the Rev. D. P. Jones says that
every missionary in the Central African Mission has to attend to many kinds of work
other than that for which he is specially sent
out, becoming teacher, carpenter, labourer, and
even cook and housekeeper by turns. The be-
ginnings of the break up of savage and furious
despotism are noticed by the missionaries. Already the permanent settlements of white men
are producing beneficial results for tribes so
long scattered and peeled by the Arabs and by
native marauders from the south and west. In
the neighbourhood of Englishmen the natives
crave for protection and feel that they have it,
as evidenced by the satisfactory progress of the
Society's work at the marine station of Kinyamkolo where a village of 400 people had been
formed, natives who were constantly under the
influence of missionary teachers.

To-day the Central African Mission has every

appearance of being thoroughly established and with reasonable expectation of enduring and successful advance. Operations for the present are limited to Urambo and the stations at the south end of the lake. So large and encouraging are the openings for a crusade among the tribes to the south and south-west of Tanganyika that they will more than occupy the forces at the Society's command. Running the gauntlet of fiery ordeals, enduring the hardships of perilous travel, surmounting obstacles of transit and malarious climates, penetrating regions untrodden by Europeans, and winning the confidence of a widening circle of natives on the route to the Lake, or inhabiting its shores, the missionaries of God hear over Tanganyika-land the strains of music, broken they may be, of the prelude :—

> "For that great harmony, whose op'ning chords
> Shall usher in the glorious coming of
> The Prince of Peace."

Slavery yet prevails in the interior of Africa. In helpless captivity lie thousands of negroes crying for strong, humane redress. It cannot be that the slave-hunters of the African Continent, regardless of the rights of humanity, will much longer be tolerated to pursue their hideously atrocious deeds unchallenged. Of the slave raider's tactics in the territories bordering on Lake Tanganyika Mr. Stanley gave a graphic narration in June, 1890, before the Manchester Chamber of Commerce, England. A thousand hired marauders each armed with a gun would march in three separate directions, "and having secured an area of 50,000 square miles they planted their flag in the centre of a village where there was a good supply of food, and here they were for three or six months. Then they began to slay in the most remorseless and cruel fashion everything having the semblance of humanity, in order to pick up what loot they could. The bananas were cut down, and men, women, and children destroyed. They slaughtered entire populations in these regions. The elephants came and completed the waste of the plantations which once nourished large populations." Upon this portraiture a frightfully realistic commentary, possibly being enacted at the time Mr. Stanley was speaking, was published in December, 1891, in Europe, through the instrumentality of that grand organisation, the African Society at Cologne.

From the diaries of several resident missionaries Canon Kespes transcribed information relative to slave-hunting in the neighbourhood of Lake Tanganyika. Under date of November 19, 1890, after a reference to the arrival of Makatubo, a villainous hunter, with a long procession of slaves at Kirando, two days' journey south of Karema, in the German sphere of influence and the departure of Father Dromaux to the spot, the diary of date, November 28, continues:

"Father Dromaux has just returned. He succeeded in liberating or buying sixty-one prisoners. A great number of their unfortunate companions have died of hunger at Kirando, and a great many more will probably soon follow them. The missionary received—partly from the slaves whom he had freed, and partly from people of the expedition—frightful details of the cruelties inflicted by Makatubo's wild hordes. During the marauding expeditions in Marungu and Kizabi innumerable natives were killed. When Makatubo set out on his march back he wished to get rid of all those who might have impeded the march; and at Lusuko, therefore, he had a great number of captives, old women and little children, drowned. The caravan was now to advance with greater haste. But a large number of captives who were completely exhausted formed a fresh hindrance. Massacres, of which one can form no idea in Europe, followed. An eyewitness assured us that daily ten, twenty, thirty, and even fifty were killed. In spite of this about 2,000 captured slaves arrived at Kirando."

This tale of horrors is confirmed by reports from a missionary at the mission station of Mpala on the western shore of Tanganyika bearing an earlier date, Sept. 8, 1890, in which it is said that a Mestizo who made a desert country westwards had, with the aid of brigands from the neighbourhood of Karema, caught in 1890 nearly 2,000 slaves, hundreds besides having been captured and slain, and the villages burnt. Another letter of date Jan. 9, from Karema, written by Father Josset, states

"that a notorious slave-hunter named Makatubo in Kirando had brought from his last expedition no less than two thousand slaves of every age and sex. They were chained together in groups of twenty to twenty-five, and looked like living skeletons. As there was a great scarcity of food in Kirando, they were forced to dig up and eat wild roots which wild animals refused to touch. Wasted away by hunger, fever and dysentery, they were sheltered in huts which afford no protection whatever against the weather. Father Dromaux told the writer that he had seen prisoners in a roofless hut ; whilst next to it their master's goats had a roof over their heads. Every morning corpses were dragged out of each hut and thrown to the hyænas. During the long march through Marungu when a slave was too exhausted to follow the caravan they killed him with cudgels."

These heart-rending accounts make it very palpable that the thousands of poor wretches, many of them women and young children happening to survive the journey across the desert with the "slave fork" lashed to their necks, are fewer in number than those who perish on their way to the coast. A letter which reached London viâ Berlin on March 26, 1892, gave fresh and graphic particulars regarding the hunt for slaves on Lake Tanganyika. The African traveller Herr Curt Ehlers at Zanzibar stated that the Portuguese travellers Senhores Diego Carmago and Peretz Elbo some weeks ago arrived in their boat at Bikari on the north-eastern shore of the lake, where they learned

that the notorious slave-hunter Makatubo, from
Kirando, had just gone on with a large number of boats to Mugo. There on the following
day the weekly market was to be held, and attended by the natives of the whole surrounding
country. Expecting some evil, the Portuguese
travellers followed, but on arriving at Mugo
were told that the small flotilla of the slave-
hunter had gone on further, leaving only one
boat there. Senhor Carmago was not deceived,
however. He bought some provisions, and
pretending to sail off, lay hidden for the whole
night in a small bay. At dawn he sent a boy to
Mugo, who brought back news that the village
had been attacked by the slave-hunters. Immediately, Senhor Carmago weighed anchor,
and the little crew, with 24 rifles, prepared the
vessel for a fight. Upon their arrival opposite
the village, the embarkation of the captured
victims, numbering about 1,500, mostly women,
was just about to begin. The slave-hunters at
first looked likely to fight, but a grenade fired
over their heads from the boat produced such
a panic amongst Makatubo's men that they

took to their heels and rushed to the boats without troubling themselves about their leader, much less about their booty. Several volleys were fired into the crowded boats. Many tried to save themselves by leaping into the lake and swimming to the shore. The inhabitants of Mugo, however, encouraged by Senhor Carmago's intervention, resolutely assailed the Arabs, and scarcely any of them escaped alive.

Another communication which Emin Pasha forwarded to his friend Dr. Fritz Finsch adds to the ghastliness of the outrages committed by the slave-marauding Arabs on the native tribes.

"North of Usongoro between the Gordon Bennett and Ruwenzori mountains," wrote Emin, "the Arab slave-raiders have had a terrible harvest. The Waganda people are their instigators here, just as the Wagala, Wabende, and the Wasissa on Lake Tanganyika. I have heard and seen terrible things on my way to the Albert lake. I followed the traces of one of these robbers, Omar Ben Chalid, for six days, and counted fifty-one fresh corpses emaciated to the bone. Thirty-nine of the victims had their skulls shattered. Twelve hundred persons are said to have been dragged to Mengo, there being twenty to thirty negroes of either sex bound to each chain. Twenty-seven, including four women, who had succeeded in escaping, met us half dead with hunger."

So far was it from being true that slavery was ended that provinces in Africa densely populated fifteen years ago, were to-day desert places, the defenceless natives having been carried off under conditions too loathsome for description. Such disclosures give significance to Lord Brougham's words spoken years back that the slave trade should be made piracy, as the only way of dealing effectually with the abomination. The opinion of Sir William Mackinnon expressed in 1890 respecting the degradation of the native races of Africa by the sale of spirituous liquors, and their destruction by the supply of guns and ammunition to the slave-hunters, ought to be laid deeply to heart by friends of the African. Says Sir William, "It is evident, that the initial and most essential step towards the regeneration and protection of the native is the absolute prohibition of all trade in these agencies of destruction." Upon this question it is surprising to note that in view of Germany's relation to the Brussels Act, certain reported transactions on her part are a direct violation of the Treaty. The London *Times* of March, 1892, had an extraordinary statement based on a letter written by Captain Stairs from Lake Tanganyika stating, " Unfortunately, he found the country flooded with gunpowder. It is imported into East Africa by the Arabs in enormous quantities with the written sanction of the German officials, and is used mainly in slave raiding and ivory stealing." It is scarcely credible that the murderous import is allowed with the sanction of the German Government in any of the provinces which fly the German flag.

Lurid as the foregoing sketches of slavery will be regarded indications are not wanting that the rescue of the negro from his present misery is being attempted on a scale not previously exhibited. Captain Lugard in Uganda and Commissioner Johnston in Nyasa-land are resisting by force the slave invasions of the Arab traders, and in the kingdom of Uganda the first mission of the Anti-Slavery League has found a home and already it has begun to make itself feared. Captain Stairs, the leader of an expedition of 1,500 men, organised by the Congo State in the interests of that State and the exploration of Katanga and, indirectly the suppression of slavery had, according to a message received in Brussels on March 10, 1892, reached Lake Tanganyika, and forthwith disbanded gangs of Arabs collected there for the purpose of making raids on the surrounding country. The extremely critical situation in 1891 on the eastern shores is becoming less strained and unsettled. About the same time Captain Hinck, following the course of the Congo, arrived on the west shore of Lake Tanganyika charged with an expedition for crushing the slave trade in Central African territories, dispersed a number of Arab chiefs and their native levies who were preparing to march on unprotected villages. Confirmatory of these tidings comes a letter from a member of a missionary society addressed to the secretary of the Anti-Slavery Society, London, dated Tanganyika, August 31, 1891, in which the writer supplements his remarks on the mode of hiring slaves at Zanzibar by saying:—" Slavery is doomed, and dying fast. Where a few years ago thousands of slaves passed my door every year *en route* for the coast, now they are reduced to hundreds, and fast becoming a non-paying article of trade. By education and trade the natives here are fast getting to that stage when men look around and claim freedom as a birthright ; and this, after all, is the only cure for slavery." He then adds : " As I have long since given my life to the snapping of the cruel chain which binds my fellows in slavery, I could not refrain from writing." Changes in regard to this horrible system cannot be wrought instantly though they will assuredly transcend all that have gone before.

In speeding that most humanizing of all enterprises, the anti-slavery cause, which Cardinal Lavigerie in Paris declared to be due to Protestant missionaries, the signs of the times in the Dark Continent are radiant with golden hopes. Africa shall live and take an " honourable place in history!" Under the wing of Christian Missions represented only by a comparative handful of souls of heroic mould, peace, good-will, self-helpfulness, industry, knowledge, commerce, government, and civilisation have been fostered and developed. By a wonderful devotion to duty of the missionary pioneers, light has been diffused, the voice of justice heard, the freedom of humanity proclaimed, and African brotherhood crowned. Notable conquests have been written across the face of Africa and on her shores magnificent feats of gallantry have been performed in the endeavour to unveil her secrets and to redeem her fettered sons and daughters. The past, so marvellous, is the promise of a great to-morrow for the consummation of which an illustrious roll of explorers and missionaries summon all nations in the ringing notes of a holy martial song of other days:

> " Here's a work of God half done,
> Here's the kingdom of His Son,
> With its triumph just begun,
> Put it through!

" For the birthright yet unsold,
For the history yet untold,
For the future yet unrolled,
    Put it through !

" 'Tis to you the trust is given,
'Tis by you the bolt is driven,
By the very God of Heaven,
    Put it through !"

www.ingramcontent.com/pod-product-compliance
Lightning Source LLC
Chambersburg PA
CBHW020351030726
47496CB00007B/2101